4.45 p.m.

Today I won four ice cream ... mate and I'm co-running, with him, a highly, successful gambling syndicate (six more people from my form now wish to join).

I don't know what more there is to life.

And I just feel very, very happy.

So why does Harvey find it all goes horribly wrong? Read on to discover the perils of being . . .
. . . a classroom gambler!

PETE JOHNSON
HELP! I'M A CLASSROOM GAMBLER

CORGI YEARLING BOOKS

HELP! I'M A CLASSROOM GAMBLER
A CORGI YEARLING BOOK 978 0 440 86627 8 (from January 2007)
0 440 86627 5

Published in Great Britain by Corgi Yearling,
an imprint of Random House Children's Books

This edition published 2006

1 3 5 7 9 10 8 6 4 2

Set in 14/15½pt Century Schoolbook
by Falcon Oast Graphic Art Ltd.

Corgi Yearling Books are published by Random House Children's Books,
61–63 Uxbridge Road, London W5 5SA,
a division of The Random House Group Ltd,
in Australia by Random House Australia (Pty) Ltd,
20 Alfred Street, Milsons Point, Sydney, NSW 2061, Australia,
in New Zealand by Random House New Zealand Ltd,
18 Poland Road, Glenfield, Auckland 10, New Zealand
and in South Africa by Random House (Pty) Ltd,
Isle of Houghton, Corner of Boundary and Carse O'Gowrie Roads,
Houghton 2198, South Africa

THE RANDOM HOUSE GROUP Limited Reg. No. 954009

www.kidsatrandomhouse.co.uk

A CIP catalogue record for this book is available from the British
Library.

Printed and bound in Great Britain by
Bookmarque Ltd, Croydon, Surrey

A WARNING TO ALL READERS

This diary is for school kids everywhere – but no one else. So it must be kept in a safe place at all times!!

Do not ever (I repeat *ever*) allow any parents or teachers to read this book – as it will only frighten them.

Thanking you in advance for your kind co-operation.

Harvey

Chapter One

WEDNESDAY JANUARY 4TH

All I did at breaktime was turn into a gorilla. And you can't tell me that's against the school rules, because it isn't.

It was a brilliant dare. The best I've ever done. A superb gorilla costume as well. A neighbour of my mate, George, had hired it and George had managed to 'borrow' it before it went back. It was dead comfortable. I reckon they should abolish our boring uniform and let us all come to school in gorilla costumes instead. We'd be so much happier.

Anyway, I lolloped off to the gym, where I swung about on the bars. Received a massive cheer as well (about half the school were watching me).

The last part of my dare was to go into the art room and grab a banana from the bowl of fruit. I thought that would be so easy and it was – until someone screamed. Very loudly.

Mrs Wadlow, the art teacher, should have been guzzling coffee in the staffroom with everyone else. Instead, she was stealing forty winks. She'd jumped awake to find an extra from *Planet of the Apes* rampaging about in her art room. So I didn't blame her at all for screaming.

That's why I said, in my most reassuring voice, 'Don't be alarmed, Mrs Wadlow. I'll just slip my head off so you can see it's only me: Harvey.'

But not even the sight of me smiling at her in an extremely friendly way could calm her down. Instead, she stuck her face right up to mine – giving me an excellent view of the moustache nestling above her lips – and screeched on and on about my outrageous behaviour.

I stood there, wishing she'd just go away and have a shave, when a sudden hush fell over everyone. This could only mean one thing – the deputy head, Mr Monslow – or

Monster as we call him – had just materialized.

He is the most terrifying teacher in the entire solar system. Darth Vader could take lessons from him in scaring people.

He's about two hundred years old, a bit hunched up, and he prowls about the school with a very sour expression on his face as if he's just swallowed something bitter. One glance at him and you'll never smile again.

'What is happening here?' he demanded in his low, mournful, undertaker's voice. Mrs Wadlow immediately accused me of . . . well just about everything, really. She even said I'd been making disgusting noises. Didn't she know anything about wildlife?

I was told to get changed, and then report to Monster's gloomy barn of a room.

I stood in front of his desk while he stared out of the window. About twenty years passed, then he slowly turned round. He's got one of those faces that are all screwed up, like a little withered apple. 'I am not at all happy,' he moaned.

Keen to strike a friendly note, I cried,

'Oh, that's a shame. Anything I can do to help?'

'I am not at all happy with your behaviour,' he hissed. 'Your name has been brought to my attention several times this year already. And now this appalling spectacle today – do you have any explanation?'

Of course I did – but not one he'd ever have understood. So I said. 'I just thought it might brighten up a new term.'

'Brighten up a new term.' He rolled the words around in his mouth, a look of deep disgust on his face. Then he gave me a double detention and said I also had to write a letter of apology to Mrs Wadlow. (For what? Waking her up!?)

'And I don't want to see you in here again,' he announced.

'Well, I can agree with you on that one,' I said with a quick laugh.

But he didn't smile back, just waggled his eyebrows at me in a highly menacing way.

4.30 p.m.
Arrived home to find Mum, Dad and Claudia (my deeply annoying sister) sitting round the kitchen table gassing

away – until I appeared. Immediately they stopped talking and all gazed at me as if I were something they'd just ordered from the shops and wished to immediately return.

Then Mum and Claudia got up and left without a word. Something was up all right. I soon discovered what it was. Monster had only rung Dad to complain about my 'appalling behaviour' today.

Dad wasn't angry or sarcastic. That's not his style. But he was so disappointed in me. 'This isn't the way to behave,' he said.

He doesn't realize: acting silly is the only way I can get through the deadly grind of school. But then, I bet Dad was a really keen pupil. Even now, whenever there's a meeting at my school he's in the front row with his little notepad, and so enthusiastic you think someone will surely give him a gold star. While Claudia (who's two years older than me) is the creepiest know-all in the whole school.

So there you have it: a family of super-swots – and me. A bit of an idiot. All right, take out the 'bit of'.

'We don't want you to throw away all your chances,' cried Dad. 'You're at a school with an excellent reputation.'

7

A few years ago it didn't even have a uniform. But then this new, whizzy headmaster took over. He's practically vanished now (you can still spot him most weeks in the local paper though, shaking hands with some businessman) but the school's become a hot ticket because of its strong sense of community (pause while I break a rib laughing) and firm discipline.

Dad said. 'Until your behaviour – and attitude – improves, I'm stopping your pocket money.'

I wasn't expecting that. 'Just because I innocently dressed up as a gorilla—' I began, indignantly.

'Please don't look on this as a punishment,' said Dad.

'What is it then?'

'A chance for you to think and change direction.'

'I could think much better with some money in my pockets,' I replied.

'Despite this little setback,' said Dad, 'we believe you have great talent; it just hasn't been channelled properly yet. We also know you won't let us down.' Then he started looking so hopeful I had to turn away.

6.15 p.m.

Dad's little pep talk had got to me. I'll admit that. And I was actually staring at a maths textbook when Claudia stormed in. Of course she knew about me dressing up as a gorilla and was absolutely furious about it (I'd brought disgrace to the family, all that lark). Then she said, 'Now, ask me what I did at school today?'

'Only if you promise not to tell me,' I replied.

'Mr Kay was explaining a maths equation on the board and then even he got stuck so I had to go up—'

'Interest level, zero,' I announced.

'I was only explaining that I'm the ideal person to make sure you do better at school in the future.' Then she actually grabbed my maths textbook.

'Put that back at once,' I growled.

'Don't be silly, Harvey, I'm helping you.'

'No you're not, because you're leaving right now. Anyway, you're only pretending to help me so Mum and Dad think you're even more wonderful than before . . . so go and show off somewhere else.'

'All right,' she sighed. 'If you're happy to be known as the class fool.'

'Yeah, that suits me just fine,' I replied.

She flounced out and moments later I heard shocked yelps from Mum and Dad as she told them what I'd said to her.

Fool. Idiot. The very naughty boy right at the back of the class. That's me. Except I don't think I am bad. Well, not really bad. It's just I find school stupendously, spectacularly, mind-blowingly DEPRESSING. Not to mention BORING. So I want to liven things up a bit. I'm a kind of human firework really: hurling a splash of colour onto the dull canvas of school by doing something totally mad.

Like a dare.

At my primary school I was the very first boy to dance like a chicken on the back field. I never looked back after that.

That same week I got inside the recycling bin and rolled down the path, while still inside it. Later that term, I climbed the Christmas tree at school, stood outside a friend's house waving a sign saying 'I'm mad', and asked a really shouty dinner lady if she'd like to marry me.

Another time I even went up to the grumpiest teacher in the school and said, 'Please, miss, I need a wee-wee.' No wonder I was known as the King of the Dares.

Then last September when I started at my new school, I met George. But I never, ever suspected we'd become brothers-in-dares.

He's half a mile smaller than me with huge, dark, grey eyes, which make him look like he's been alive for at least two hundred years. He's extremely serious too – walks around frowning all the time. But one day after school, he left his mobile phone behind on the sweet counter. I went after him and we got talking.

We discovered that we both liked bird-watching, reading and eating chocolate. In fact, we had so much in common. So we spent more and more time together. George is very deep. I like that in a friend. But he doesn't know much about the ways of school . . . unlike me. So I look out for him and now we just seem to belong together like – bacon and eggs.

Of course I told George all about my 'dares'. He was highly impressed but he thought the word 'dares' was a bit childish. He thought we should call ourselves . . . 'Chancers'.

And I'm now doing much more sophisticated things. For instance, speaking with an Italian accent for two whole lessons so the supply teacher really believed I was Italian.

We spend ages planning our challenges too and keep them top secret until the day.

I'm cooking up a challenge for George for next Monday. He was asking me about it tonight. But I refused to even give him a clue.

I just said that it's going to be totally brilliant.

Chapter Two

Redundant teachers ↓ ↓

THURSDAY JANUARY 5TH

Ways to improve school:

1. Play good music when we arrive.

2. Get all the teachers to stand in a line and wait to be picked by the pupils. The teachers who no one wants are sent home and a fresh supply brought in.

3. Lessons can only last for twenty minutes. No one can listen to a teacher for any longer than that.

4. Teachers have got to say something good to you every day, even if it's just 'Well done for tucking your shirt in.'

5. No school uniform – far too ugly.

6. No homework – we work hard enough at school.

7. Schools shouldn't make you work every single day. That's just not natural. At least twice a week you should be allowed to bring games in and enjoy yourself.

7.15 p.m.
Guess what? I've just locked my sister out of the house! I can hear her hammering away on the front door as I write this. But it's her own fault.

You see, Mum and Dad have gone out to a meeting at school and said they were leaving Claudia in charge. Of course this new power went straight to her head.

I was just quietly raiding the kitchen when she started moaning at me. 'Oh, you know we've only just bought that cake. You can't have too much of it now. And you shouldn't be filling up on cakes and sweets anyhow . . .'

A few minutes later I was doing a bit of homework on the kitchen floor (I work better when I'm lying down) and she came barging in again. 'Oh Harvey, sit up at the kitchen table and do your homework properly.'

'I'm fine here, thanks,' I said.

'But your handwriting's messy enough normally. You want your teacher to be able to read it, don't you?'

'Not bothered,' I replied. 'And stop harassing me – you'll be asking me if I've been to the toilet next.'

'I'm only trying to help,' she whined.

'Claudia, you're not my mother.'

'Thank goodness,' she cried. 'But I am, at the moment, head of the household.'

'You're not in charge of me.'

'I think you'll find I am, actually. And I am telling you to do your homework properly on the kitchen table.'

'Go on then, make me,' I challenged.

She gave a cry of exasperation and stormed off.

I moved upstairs to my bedroom where a few minutes later she appeared yet again, this time with a black bin bag.

'Any rubbish in here?' she asked.

'Only you.'

'I'm trying to clean up to help our parents.'

'Oh, have five gold stars. You're so perfect you bring me out in a rash.'

'And your room stinks.' She started opening a window,

'Hey, stop that.'

'No I won't. You need some fresh air in here. Now, leave it open.'

Of course as soon as she'd left I slammed the window shut again. Then I heard her putting the rubbish out. And well, I just couldn't resist it. I hurtled downstairs – and locked both the front and back doors.

She's shouting at me through the letter-box now. When do you think I should let her in? Midnight? No, that's far too soon.

8.30 p.m.
I let her back in at eight o'clock.

I know. I'm just too soft hearted.

But she wasn't at all grateful. Instead, she went squawking about the place saying. 'Just wait until Mum and Dad find out what you've done.'

Oh, I'm so scared.

Then I heard her on the phone to Gemma – the one girl who's nearly as demented as she is. She said. 'Harvey's hopeless you know, useless at everything. It's so embarrassing having him for a brother. I've tried to help him. Not any more though. He and I are sworn enemies now.'

I thought we were anyhow.

FRIDAY JANUARY 6TH

Three teachers are away with flu. But none of them teach me. Talk about inconsiderate.

George's parents split up over Christmas. So now he spends the weekdays with his mum and the weekends with his dad (and nan) and he's getting sick of it. He said, 'I think I should just stay in one house and my parents move in and out.'

SUNDAY JANUARY 8TH

12.15 p.m.

A bit earlier, Claudia came into the kitchen and declared, 'I've got something to say to you, Harvey.' Then there was this lengthy pause.

'Well hurry up, I'm growing a beard here waiting,' I said.

'I think it's silly us not talking,' she began.

'I don't . . . I think it's great.'

'And I'd like us to make up,' she continued in this stiff, little voice.

Before I could reply Mum and Dad popped up; they must have been hiding behind the door all the time. 'Now that's what we like to hear,' said Dad.

Claudia beamed at Mum and Dad. I'd already guessed her little speech was just to please them.

'Now would you like to give your sister a hug?' asked Mum.

'Take a wild guess, Mum,' I replied, folding my arms.

'It's so good that you two have made up your differences,' said Dad.

A few minutes later I was in my bedroom when Claudia stuck her head round the door. 'Just to let you know I still utterly despise you.'

'Sssh, Mum and Dad might hear and think you're not totally wonderful after all.'

'Some sisters have brothers they can talk to—'

'No boy would ever want to talk to you,' I interrupted. 'For a start, you've got breath that could kill an elephant.'

'You think you're just so funny,' she cried. 'But you're not . . . you're pathetic. The school idiot.'

'At least I'm not my parents' little pet. Oh no, they haven't called you "wonderful" for at least ten minutes. What will you do?'

Claudia didn't say another word. Instead she started practising on her flute.

18

She knows that sets my teeth on edge. So she went on for hours.

7.00 p.m.
George has just returned from his dad's house. 'All weekend Dad and Nan have been making these snide, little cracks about Mum. Now, it's Mum's turn to say bad stuff about him. I can't believe they're acting like this. They should be setting me an example.'

I agreed that they should.

'They said when they split up that they'd get on much better. That's a laugh. They're still as mad as ever at each other – only in different houses.'

I advised him to forget all about his parents – and just think about the challenge I've got for him tomorrow.

He still hasn't a clue what it's about.

Chapter Three

MONDAY JANUARY 9TH

2.30 p.m.
DISASTER!

Still can't believe what's happened.

Just before double history, the last lesson of the day, I said to George, 'The moment of truth has arrived. Your challenge in history is to turn yourself into someone who's just been attacked by a mad vampire ... This will help you,' I added, handing him a bottle of fake blood. 'You just have to sit in history with blood dripping down your face and a look of complete horror in your eyes.'

'What a top challenge!' said George.

'I know,' I said.

I'd picked history, because you can have a laugh with the teacher, Mr Smart. Also, he lets you in the classroom when he's not there. So we rushed in and George immediately began dabbing 'blood' on his jaw. It was quite thick – like treacle – but astonishingly realistic, especially from a distance. Soon 'blood' was running all down George's neck and splattering onto his desk and books. The rest of the class was in hysterics. A couple of girls even pretended to shriek with horror. But George didn't look scared enough. In fact, he kept laughing madly – until the door opened and silence swept into the room.

'I can hear you all the way down the corridor,' whispered Monster (he's the only teacher who never has to raise his voice). 'You know you must wait for Mr Smart – in silence.'

Poor George was lowering his head like a tortoise retreating into its shell, just hoping Monster wouldn't notice him. But all at once, he did.

Monster gave this little jump as if he'd just received an electric shock. For a moment he'd actually thought it was real blood and that made me smile a little.

But then he pointed a large, bony finger at George and said, very softly – the madder he is, the quieter he speaks – 'You, lad, to my room now.'

George got up, 'blood' still streaming down his face. Only now there really was a look of complete horror in his eyes.

3.15 p.m.
End of school – but no sign of George. Is he still in Monster's room?

What's going on?

3.45 p.m.
I've just visited Monster's secretary in her little glass office. I was extra polite too. I said. 'I do hope you are feeling well. Could you kindly inform me if George Talbot is still being held for questioning?'

But she just stared down her nose at me and told me to stop wasting her time. Couldn't she see I was in a highly agitated state?

3.55 p.m.
I'm *still* waiting for George!!

4.10 p.m.
Sighted George at last. Just saw him

staggering out of Monster's lair. The blood had hardened on his chin now. It was all over his hands too. He looked as if he'd been in a bad accident. His mum was with him.

'So what's happened?' I demanded.

He could only make a strange, little noise in his throat. Spending all that time with Monster had clearly traumatized him.

'I'm afraid we haven't got time to talk now,' snapped his mum, giving me this evil glare.

Then she rushed George away from me.

7.00 p.m.
George has just rung.

'I don't want my mum to hear me,' he whispered.

'Actually, I can hardly hear you,' I replied.

Raising his voice he told me how Monster blamed the whole incident on me. He said I'd infected George with my bad ways.

Then he sent for George's mum.

You really won't believe what I'm going to tell you next. Monster said it'd be best if George and me were separated in all our lessons.

All this hassle over a few innocent drops of fake blood.

This has been a dead, horrible day.

TUESDAY JANUARY 10TH

4.00 p.m.

Those lousy, rotten teachers have got George and me sitting so far away, we're practically in different rooms now. Even at breaktime a teacher was stalking us. This is nothing less than pupil harassment.

All day I kept shouting jokes to George and sending him stupid messages. I'm worn out from being so cheerful.

9.30 p.m.

Tried ringing George several times tonight but his phone was permanently switched off.

WEDNESDAY JANUARY 11TH

10.45 a.m.

I saw George at breaktime (wasn't permitted to talk to him, of course). He was walking along on his own, misery coming off him like steam.

He gets very depressed sometimes. And I'm the only person who can cheer him up.

1.40 p.m.
Just returned from a secret meeting with George. Beyond the back field there are some woods, totally out of bounds. We both slipped through a gap in the fence and met up under a huge oak tree.

He told me that his dad came round last night. Of course his parents had a big row about George falling into bad company. (Yes, that's me, folks!) Then his dad suggested confiscating George's mobile.

For a few seconds I was speechless with shock. A mobile phone is one of life's essentials. Taking that away is like stopping someone drinking water or eating chocolate. 'I didn't think parents were allowed to be so barbaric,' I cried.

'Oh they are,' said George, grimly. 'So now when I'm at home I shall be totally cut off from all civilization.'

8.30 p.m.
Took a chance tonight. Told my parents about George and me being split up – hoping they'd write an official letter of protest. Instead, they just went on and on about the fake blood. Honestly, adults have no sense of proportion.

Of course my sister didn't help by saying,

'I told you Harvey's a total nightmare. I'm the laughing stock of the school having him for a brother.'

'We really hoped you were making a fresh start, Harvey, after our little chat,' said Dad, his voice quivering with disappointment.

9.35 p.m.
George has just called. He'd managed to sneak out of his house to ring me from a smelly, old phone box. I said, 'We'll be using pigeons to communicate with each other next.'

Tonight George told his mum, 'Let me have my mobile back and I promise when you're old I'll put you into a very nice nursing home.'

But his mum even turned down that generous offer.

Things are now looking very serious indeed.

Chapter Four

Putrid SNOT filled germ cloud

SNIFF

THURSDAY JANUARY 12TH

This morning I yelled, 'It's snowing. Massive big flakes as well.' Everyone piled to the window, even the teacher. I'd have given anything if it really had been.

Today just crawled past. I don't know who's more fed-up, George or me. We're a double act. And on my own, it's as if some vital part of me is missing.

Five teachers are now away with flu – but all mine are disgustingly healthy. Sometimes life can be so unfair. Still, they said on the news tonight that a flu epidemic could be starting, so I suppose that's something to look forward to.

FRIDAY JANUARY 13TH

Definitely an unlucky Friday 13th today with double maths, a spot history test and an English lesson so excruciatingly dull I nearly fell asleep. Added to which, all these George-less days have driven me to take desperate action. Today I went up to this boy who's got a very runny nose. In fact, it was running so fast it could have entered races. His eyes were streaming too.

'You look full of flu,' I said.

He nodded grimly.

'Well, breathe on me for about five minutes, will you?' He proved extremely helpful. And having performed this good deed he went off to see Matron and left school shortly afterwards. So he must have been positively teeming with germs. Perfect!

Later I managed to snatch a few words with George.

I said, 'I think it's best if I let things calm down here a bit. So I shall be away next week.'

'But how will you manage that?' he asked.

'An attack of flu – coming up very shortly.'

There was no time to say anything else so George just hissed, 'Get well soon, won't you?'

SATURDAY JANUARY 14TH

Any moment now the flu will kick in. I'm looking forward to a week in bed, as I love reading. I can sit down and read a book from cover to cover. Well, I'll have loads of time for that next week.

SUNDAY JANUARY 15TH

The flu is taking its time. Not so much as a sore throat yet.

MONDAY JANUARY 16TH

7.55 a.m.

I am completely healthy and full of despair. I could, of course, pretend to be ill. But Mum will only slam a thermometer in my mouth and ask about two million questions. Maybe the flu will kick in when I get up. Maybe I'll collapse on the way to the bathroom. Here's hoping.

8.05 a.m.

No such luck.

Another diabolically rubbish week awaits me.

9.25 a.m.

School Assembly.

Two of the most boring words in the English language. And we have assemblies every single day here. Don't ask me why. You never learn anything – except how to sleep with your eyes open.

All Years Seven, Eight and Nine are packed into the Sports Hall. Only everyone has to take their shoes off first. So this awful pong of cheese that's been left out in the sun too long wafts over you and nearly brings up your breakfast.

Then you're jammed onto this cold, hard floor (I get cramp afterwards every single day) while the teachers hiss and spit at you to 'Look to the front' and 'Be quiet'.

When everyone's crammed in, one of the teachers goes and stands in front of the doors with his arms folded like a bouncer. And you think, that's it, I'm sealed in here for at least twenty minutes.

Only it's more like thirty minutes if it's a Monster assembly, which it was today. All the teachers were especially jittery (they're even more scared of him than we are). One even snapped at me, 'You boy, breathe more quietly.'

Well, that set off one of my laughing

spasms, didn't it? I just couldn't stop; so then I had to get up and was sent to sit with Year Nine at the back of the hall. I saw Claudia turn away in horror as I drew near. 'Hi ya, sis? How's it grooving?' I called out. She put her head in her hands. I nearly sat next to her, just to maximize her embarrassment. But in the end I plonked myself beside Jonny.

Everyone knows him. He's been in the paper because of his amazing football skill – now he's having a trial for a football club. A really top one as well, though don't ask me which one. Yet Jonny never swaggers around the school. Instead, he just seems amused by everything. He's always got this crazy little twinkle in his eye, as if right now there's a party going on in his head.

He grinned at me. 'What are you in trouble for now?'

'Breathing too loudly.'

'You rebel,' he said.

And then a deathly chill fell upon the room as Monster strode quickly to the lectern, his eyes darting about all the time. For ages he didn't speak, and all you could hear were his bones creaking. Then he had some shocking news. School was suffering from an outbreak of . . . trainers.

He ranted on and on about this, filling you with a gloom that hangs over you for the rest of the day like a massive, grey cloud.

After he'd gone, Mr Cummings, the head of Year Seven, stepped forward. He's a small, very tired-looking man, who inserts massive pauses into the middle of his sentences. 'From this moment,' he said, 'all trainer-wearing must stop. Teachers will be patrolling the . . . er . . . er . . . school to check you are not wearing er . . .'

'Bananas.'

That just popped out. Luckily none of the teachers heard me, but the Year Nines I was sitting with did. And it really cheered them up. Jonny even repeated 'Bananas' in a highly appreciative way too.

Couldn't help feeling a little proud.

12.35 p.m.

In English we were looking at this extract from *Treasure Island* by Robert Louis Stevenson. I've read the book and watched two different film versions. So I was saying all this stuff about what a great character that Long John Silver was and being dead fascinating. Or so I thought. Only the teacher suddenly said, 'Harvey, will you look at the board and read out today's lesson objective.'

So I read, 'Today's lesson objective is to look at the different ways you can start a sentence.'

Then she said in this very thin-lipped way, 'So will you please confine your comments to that?'

I never said another word. Then I got this note from George: *Are you trying to become swot of the year?*

I wrote back: *You have discovered my guilty secret. But what are my chances of being swot of the year? Nil, I'd say.*

George's reply was: *Swot of the Year Challenge. I bet I can ask more questions in history than you this afternoon. Do you care to accept this challenge?*

I certainly did. More notes passed as we worked out the rules. The teacher had got to think the questions were genuine. If he told you to shut up you'd be disqualified. We also decided there should be a prize – one ice cream.

3.50 p.m.
The History Challenge.
Exclusive Match report – by *Harvey*.
The game began with a storming

performance by me. Ladies and gentlemen, I was on fire: 'Can we switch on the light?' 'Do you want the board cleaned?' No question was too puerile for me. No wonder I took an early lead (6–0).

But once the lesson started properly I was totally outclassed. I may have a lot of cheek but George has brains. And in the end, unfortunately, brains won out.

I tried to recover with probing questions about whether Mr Smart preferred teaching in the morning or afternoon. But it was hopeless. My final score was a miserable 9 against George's utterly triumphant 17.

Afterwards George couldn't stop grinning. We were off to get his prize when he spotted his mum. She was waiting at the school gates for him.

'Oh no,' he moaned. 'I told her I didn't want a lift home. She's only doing this to spy on me.'

'And check you're not fraternizing with the enemy: me,' I said.

George nodded grimly.

In secret I watched him trudge over to his mum. He looked like a prisoner being escorted off the premises by a guard.

TUESDAY JANUARY 17TH

9.00 a.m.

Passed George a note on which I'd written: *I owe you one ice cream. Any flavour you wish . . . Harvey.* We'd also decided to have a re-match in maths.

Mr Kay, the maths teacher, is a huge man with half a nose and a very uncertain temper. He can turn into a raving loony in the blink of an eye. And when he gets mad his whole body shakes with fury. His nickname is Wobblebottom.

Anyway, he didn't like us asking him all these questions. In fact, he quickly went a bit frothy at the mouth. So we stopped immediately.

Then he was writing something on the board. Only every so often he'd stop to give himself a scratch under his arms. He really dug around in there too. I'm sure he's got fleas.

All at once an idea scorched through my brain. I hastily scribbled a note to George: *I bet Wobblebottom will scratch his armpits seven more times before the bell goes. What do you bet?*

I waited impatiently for my note to reach George (postal service in this classroom could definitely be speedier), then

George gave me a big grin and mouthed 'Five' at me.

Our eyes never left Wobblebottom for the rest of the lesson. He managed four, vigorous scratches nice and easily. But we had to wait ages for the fifth one. After that it really looked as if George had won. Homework had been set. The bell was about to go . . .

Suddenly, right out of the blue, Wobblebottom stood up and scratched himself: TWICE. Immediately afterwards the bell went. So, just when I'd given up all hope Wobblebottom had come through for me. Now I know how those punters feel when the horse they've bet on suddenly gallops forward out of nowhere and wins the race.

I went up to Wobblebottom, beaming with joy. 'Just wanted to say congratulations on a top lesson, sir. In fact, I'd say it's your best one ever.'

Wobblebottom looked at me in a puzzled sort of way for a couple of seconds. Then he smiled which was very unusual and kind of scary.

Even though he'd lost, George was jubilant. He whispered to me afterwards. 'That wasn't the usual, dead old maths lesson. We turned it on its head. We took charge. We *owned* that lesson.'

4.15 p.m.
At the end of school George slipped off with me to buy our prize-winning ice creams. He said his mum would just have to wait. He was still really high from our challenge in maths. I felt intoxicated with delight too.

The ice-cream van is just down the road from our school. It sells masses of other stuff too. And it was swarming with customers, as usual. 'Even a normal ice cream tastes great,' said George. 'But when you've won one, it tastes fantastic.'

'Bit cold for ice creams, isn't it?' asked Jonny.

'I'd eat ice creams in a blizzard,' I replied.

Jonny looked at us. 'What are you two so happy about anyway?'

It was flattering having Jonny start up a conversation with me. So I told him what had happened in maths. He was highly amused.

8.30 p.m.
In what other lessons could George and me have a little flutter? I've been sitting in

my bedroom doing some deep thinking on this very subject.

Here's what I've come up with so far:

Art: Mrs Wadlow is a keen gulper. Really deep gulps too, as if she's doing an impression of a turkey.

French: How often the teacher says 'Well'. He is very attached to this word.

Metalwork: How many minutes before sweat patches start appearing under the teacher's arms?

P.E. The number of times he calls us 'son' or 'sunshine?'

I was just working on a brilliant bet for geography, when Mum popped in with a cup of tea for me. She assumed I was doing homework and gave me a pleased smile.

Of course, I'm actually working on something much more important than mere homework.

Chapter Five

WEDNESDAY JANUARY 18TH

George and me had a brilliant flutter this afternoon. We bet on the number of times our geography teacher would blow his nose.

His nose-blowing is the highlight of every lesson. He produces this big hankie with a mighty flourish, just as if he's about to do a conjuring trick. And he really peers at the hankie as if it's got a secret message hidden somewhere on it. Then he buries his nose right into it and makes these loud, trumpeting noises, like the mating call of a lovesick elephant.

A showstopper every time!

He's also got bushels of hair up his nose. And afterwards you can often see little bits of hankie dangling off them. A revolting sight – but in a really good way.

Anyway, I bet on him blowing his nose three times, but George, to my great surprise, only opted for one nose blow. Yet George was exactly right. He told me afterwards he'd taken into account the time of day, and how the peak time for nose-blowing is usually the morning. I had completely overlooked this vital fact.

I told you George was clever, didn't I? His excellent deduction showed just how much skill these bets require. They're highly educational, actually.

George was so disappointed that he couldn't collect his ice cream after school. But his mum had made such a big fuss about him being so late yesterday that he didn't dare risk her wrath again.

'Parents shouldn't be allowed to give you lifts when you don't want them,' I said. 'It's nothing less than kidnapping.'

I handed him an I OWE YOU and George told me he is now keeping a detailed record of all our bets.

THURSDAY JANUARY 19TH

Two more bets today. In French, the teacher broke all records with the number of times he said 'Well.' A truly magnificent score of twenty-six. George was closest (betting on twenty).

Then we had a re-match in Wobble-bottom's lesson. This time he managed seven scratches (I won that one again).

The rest of the class wanted to know what we were doing. So I told them. It's no big secret. And as I expected, they sniggered and said we were 'totally mad'.

But I just replied, 'I couldn't care less what you think. George and me are having a better time in lessons than you are, and that's all that matters.'

I'm right too, aren't I?

FRIDAY JANUARY 20TH

Saw Jonny today. He was in the middle of this huge group of Year Nines – even my sister was hanging about in the background. But when he spotted me he left all of them to have a chat. The coolest boy in the school wanted to talk to its biggest idiot. How about that? My sister's eyes were just hanging out. Jonny wanted to know more about the 'secret bets'. He

41

laughed a lot when I told him about the nose-blowing bet in geography. He thought that was hilarious – but highly ingenious too.

When he went off he said, 'See you then, Harvey,' just as if he and I were mates.

I called back. 'See you, Jonny,' very loudly, so my sister, who was still hovering about, could hear.

SATURDAY JANUARY 21ST

Claudia's spoken to me for the first time in ages. She wanted to know what Jonny and me were talking about.

'Oh, we're always conversing,' I said. 'Jonny just enjoys my superb company.'

'Well, if you're just going to be silly,' said Claudia.

'All right then,' I said, 'I'll tell you the truth. He was asking me about you.'

I just said that as a silly joke. But talk about bigheaded. She actually *believed* me. And she was gazing at me really keenly now. So I went on, 'I told him sisters are a really bad mistake and best avoided – especially mine.'

Then Claudia looked as if she was about to combust. While I just laughed and laughed.

SUNDAY JANUARY 22ND

Guess what? I've got my pocket money back. Dad said that over the last few days he'd noticed a definite change in my attitude. 'I feel you're really starting to get something out of school now.'

'You're exactly right, Dad,' I replied. 'In fact, I've never enjoyed it more.'

MONDAY JANUARY 23RD

12.35 p.m.
Just had the best lesson of my entire life! Sends a tingle down my spine just thinking about it.

Seven teachers were away with flu today, including Wobblebottom! So we had this supply teacher, Mr Barker (he wrote his name in big letters on the board). He'd obviously dressed with care: smart tweed jacket, dignified tie and tie pin, rather magnificent cufflinks. He was small with a grizzled little moustache and glasses which hung on a chain round his neck. He kept peering at us through them in some bewilderment. I think he was used to posher schools than ours. But he had beautiful manners. He practically bowed when you asked him something and spoke to us ever so politely. He said, 'Now I expect you'd like to know something about me first, wouldn't you?'

We all chorused 'Yes' (anything to waste time).

He told us how he'd retired from teaching, then found he wasn't ready to be put out to pasture quite yet, so he was keeping his hand in with a spot of supply work.

'Now, please bear with me if I don't remember all your names right away, but I promise you I will try.'

Then he started fumbling in his bag for some notes he'd been given. 'Now, please bear with me,' he repeated. Then he found his notes but still kept looking around him like an actor who isn't quite sure of his lines and is waiting to be prompted.

He was a funny old boy, but kind of likeable. Only I couldn't see him lasting long in this school. In fact, he was going to get slaughtered.

And then something happened. Suddenly his whole head just shook and he released the most magnificent twitch I'd ever seen. Everyone gaped at him in total wonderment. After which he gave a second, equally magnificent twitch. And immediately afterwards his moustache started shifting about, as if it suddenly had a life of its own.

It was quite incredible to watch. And everyone just forgot about misbehaving as they eagerly awaited the next twitch.

Unfortunately, it was only a single period. So George and I didn't really have time to get a proper bet going. But tomorrow . . . he had to be back tomorrow. At the end of the lesson I sped up to him.

He was already pouring out tea from a small flask and unwrapping some egg sandwiches. 'There is no objection to me eating my sandwiches in here, is there? I know they do give off a slight odour.'

'You eat away,' I said airily, giving him permission with a wave of my hand.

'May I offer you one?' he asked.

'Another time, maybe . . .' I said. 'Actually, I was just wondering if you'd be back tomorrow?'

'Oh yes, they think Mr Kay will be away for some time, I'm afraid. He's proper poorly.'

Now I was so happy I could hardly speak. 'See you tomorrow then, Mr Twi— Barker.'

'You will indeed, young man,' he replied. 'And thanks for your interest.'

'No, thank you, sir,' I replied.

1.05 p.m.
Interest is certainly growing in Chancer, the gambling syndicate (as people now call it). George and me have just been answering all these questions about it.

'I can't see the point of it,' said one girl.

'All right, answer me this,' I replied. 'When was the last time you ever found a lesson too exciting?'

Everyone laughed at the very idea.

'Well, I left geography last Wednesday with my heart pounding away. I couldn't have been more excited if . . . I'd been chased by a whole squad of killer wasps.'

'Yet it really relaxes you as well,' chipped in George. 'Makes you forget all your worries.'

Well, two boys want to join us. I wasn't surprised by Tyrone's interest; he is the kind of boy who has to be in on everything. Yet Lee's much quieter and not someone I'd have expected to be keen at all. But should George and me open up Chancer to other people?

1.15 p.m.
A girl's just smiled at me. That doesn't

46

happen very often (I've got a face like a potato). She's the most attractive girl in my class too. Her name's Ellen . . . And I'm still in a state of shock about the whole incident, to be honest. Anyway, she wishes to be part of the syndicate too.

1.35 p.m.
Just back from a private meeting with George. A split decision at first. I was keen to open up Chancer to new members but George really wasn't. He felt it would stop being special if we let other people in. I argued it could make things even more exciting. And of course the winner would now take away with him four ice creams . . . an eye-popping prize by any standards. In the end I persuaded George. He said I'd answered all his misgivings.

But I agreed with him we had to make things more official. We were like a small business now. So I'm going to make some Chancer cards on the computer.

4.30 p.m.
Thought you'd like to see one of the new Chancer cards. So here it is:

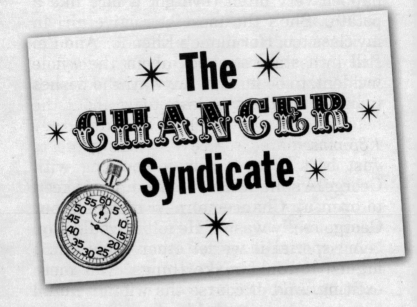

The **CHANCER** Syndicate

TUESDAY JANUARY 24TH

8.00 a.m.

Drew back the curtains to see a grey mist hanging over everything. Normally that would look highly depressing. But today it didn't. Instead, it made everything seem mysterious and dream-like, as if anything could happen. And it might. For this is the day we've opened up Chancer to new members. Who knows where that might lead?

Feel as if a whole new story could be starting for me.

12.30 p.m.

Twitcher didn't need to ask for silence. From the moment he arrived everyone was gazing at him with the keenest interest. The whole class knew about the bets we'd placed on Twitcher. And they were fascinated to see who was going to win.

And Twitcher didn't disappoint. He gave a dramatic twitch the moment he started talking as if to say: 'I'm on top form today.'

A boy behind me whispered, 'Is it too late to join the syndicate?'

Regretfully, I had to inform him that no bets could be accepted once the game was underway.

The atmosphere was just intoxicating. And talk about tense. The bets were so close together that right until the final moment it could have been anyone's game.

Then, just before the bell rang he gave a truly, magnificent double twitch, clinching victory for . . . *me*. My head nearly fell off with joy.

4.45 p.m.

Today I won four ice creams. I've also got a top mate and I'm co-running, with him, a highly successful gambling syndicate (six more people from my form now wish to join).

I don't know what more there is to life. And I just feel very, very happy.

Chapter Six

WEDNESDAY JANUARY 25TH

11.45 a.m.

Twitchy told us he likes teaching our class best. And it shows. He's the most awesome teacher we've ever had. Today he even set a new record: twenty-nine twitches in one lesson. He never lets us down.

Ellen won today. I said, 'You're obviously a born gambler.' And we had a bit of a laugh together. Then she said how Chancer was a 'genius idea'.

'Say any more and I'll start blushing,' I grinned.

George and me haven't decided yet whether to expand the syndicate still further to eleven. We're going to have another private meeting at lunchtime. So many teachers are away we can hang around together at break and lunchtimes now without anyone bothering us. As I said to George, 'I knew we'd win in the end.'

1.30 p.m.
George and me have just faced our first crisis.

Tyrone told us he would be unable to buy Ellen an ice cream after school, as he was 'flat broke'.

'But why didn't you tell us before?' I demanded.

Tyrone went very red indeed. It was not a pretty sight. He knew he'd behaved in a squalid way.

'It's not just the ice cream you owe Ellen today,' I said. 'Your debt will go on rising – three ice creams by Friday.'

'Unless I win,' he said.

I liked his spirit, but I didn't see how he could remain in the syndicate. Neither did George. 'If we let him get away with it . . .' he began, 'Well, that's how anarchy starts.'

This was true, but I really didn't want to chuck him out. That seemed against the fun-spirit of Chancer. Then I had a suggestion. Instead of buying Ellen an ice cream, maybe Tyrone could be her servant for a day.

'That's a truly, brilliant solution,' said George. 'However did you think of it?'

'I don't exactly know,' I replied. 'For years I've had all these ideas roaming about in my head – they just never found a way out before.'

8.30 p.m.
Just discovered my parents in this huddle in the kitchen, whispering away. They had to be talking about me. For one ghastly, gut-wrenching moment I thought they'd found out about the syndicate. But, no; if they knew about that they'd be having forty fits.

They looked up at me in a rather guilty way, I thought. Then they gave me these glassy smiles, which disturbed me greatly. 'So how's everything in Harvey's world today?' asked Dad in a far too-cheerful voice.

'Good, good,' I said vaguely, wondering what they were up to now. Parents really are a constant worry.

4.05 p.m.

Tyrone was waiting at the school gates for Ellen this morning. He bowed and said. 'Good morning, ma'am, may I be permitted to carry your bag?'

Got into his part right away.

He carried Ellen's bag around all day for her. Also, he took out her pens and pencils and arranged them very neatly at the start of every lesson.

Then at lunchtime, while Ellen reclined at her table, Tyrone queued up to get her food. Ellen grinned at me and said, 'I could get used to this.' That's three times in a week she's smiled at me. It's getting to be a habit!

The servant-for-a-day option will now be a regular alternative to ice cream.

George and me have agreed to expand Chancer to eleven members. But George thinks that is the absolute maximum now. He also believes we should have proper membership cards, on which we must put a © for copyright and a little message pointing out that this is totally our invention.

6.30 p.m.
May I present the Chancer membership cards:

LICENSE TO GAMBLE© MEMBER

Signature _____

Chancer No: _____

George and Harvey are the sole (and brilliant) inventors of 'License to Gamble' and any one who says otherwise will suffer huge freaky bad luck!!

9.15 p.m.
Just heard Mum knock on Claudia's door. 'Is there anything you want to talk to us about, love?' she asked.

Claudia replied in this funny, muffled voice. 'No, I'm absolutely fine, honestly. I just want to be on my own for a bit.'

Mum ignored this and popped in any-way, though. Couldn't catch much of what they were saying, because they were talking dead softly. But at one point Mum's voice rose sharply. 'Claudia, we feel something is wrong. And you know you can tell us anything. So what's happened, love?'

Were my ears dreaming? Was creepy, goody, swotty Claudia actually in trouble? I couldn't make out what Claudia said in reply but it obviously didn't satisfy Mum because she gave this loud sigh of disappointment before huffing off.

So it must have been Claudia my parents were discussing last night. What a relief! And isn't it great that she's in trouble and not me. I wonder what's she's done.

Here's hoping it's something sensationally bad.

FRIDAY JANUARY 27TH

12.30 p.m.
Tragic news. Even though Wobblebottom will not be back on Monday, this is Twitcher's last day. Whole class is still in a state of shock.

Twitcher said he'd never met a class with such advanced listening skills. 'Nothing ever distracts you,' he said wonderingly. 'You keep your eyes fixed on me for the entire lesson. If only the rest of the school was as attentive.' There'd been riots in all his other classes.

At the end of the lesson I told him how greatly he would be missed. His face shook with emotion and he released one of his magnificent double twitches.

A class act right up to the end.

SATURDAY JANUARY 28TH
5.30 p.m.
It's all kicking off here.

Would you believe my mum and Claudia have just had a massive row? Then Dad joined in (on Mum's side) I'm not completely sure of all the facts yet. But it seems as if Mum found Claudia's diary and had a sneaky look through it. Claudia discovered her doing this and went completely mad. She actually screamed at Mum.

Of course, Mum screamed back that she thought Claudia had left the diary lying about as a cry for help. I'm just loving all this, of course. In fact, it's brightened up my Saturday afternoon no end. And it's not over yet. More rows to follow, I hope.

6.15 p.m.

Dad went upstairs to talk to Claudia to try and calm her down. Meanwhile, Mum was looking so miserable I made her a cup of tea and inisisted she eat a slice of cake for energy. 'Rowing with my sister's dead exhausting,' I said. 'And I should know. I'm an expert.'

Mum ate two slices of cake and told me she wouldn't normally have read the diary, but she's been very worried about Claudia lately. She said Claudia just hasn't been herself. She's been quiet and withdrawn. She asked me if I'd noticed anything. 'Not a thing,' I replied. 'She just seemed her usual, highly annoying self to me.'

I asked Mum what was in Claudia's diary. She refused to even give me a hint. She said it wouldn't be fair. 'I'm only enquiring so I can help Claudia,' I said. Mum actually laughed then.

9.30 p.m.

I've found out a bit more about Claudia's diary. I just happened to overhear Mum and Dad talking about it! Apparently, Claudia's very, very worried about her schoolwork and whether she will stay top of the class! There are pages and pages of her bleating on about this . . . and nothing else.

Trust my sister to keep the most boring diary in the entire solar system! Now if Mum and Dad ever got their hands on the diary you are reading now, well, they'd just get the shock of their lives, wouldn't they?

My diary is red-hot. That's why I keep it beside me at all times.

SUNDAY JANUARY 29TH

The fun's over. Claudia's made up with Mum and Dad. Lots of tears and hugs and all that silly slobber. Now they are all downstairs having a lovely chat about the pressures of being a brainbox. Trust me to grow up in a house crawling with super-swots. It's just lucky I've got a strong personality, otherwise I could feel a right turnip head.

MONDAY JANUARY 30TH

1.30 p.m.
Took bets today in French. But some of the magic had gone. We were all missing Twitchy so much. And when you've seen the best, someone saying 'Well' (even if it was twenty-seven times − a new record)

59

seems a poor substitute.

I set up a petition signed by every single person in my class, demanding that Twitchy returns. I handed it to Mr Cummings. I thought he'd be pleased we were taking an interest in school staffing. Instead, he was highly suspicious. 'Why are you . . . erm, doing this?' he asked.

'We just think he's a belting teacher and we'd like him back . . . by tomorrow, if you can manage that.'

I am not at all hopeful.

4.00 p.m.
Ellen won ten ice creams today; only she was allowed other confectionery options like chocolate and sweets as well. She asked if instead of buying her an ice cream I'd like to be her servant for a day. I said yes a little too eagerly, I fear. But a girl has never asked me to be her servant for a day before. So it's a big moment in my life.

TUESDAY JANUARY 31ST
9.00 a.m.
Ellen cycles to school every morning. I was waiting for her. But I was cool this time. I didn't say very much – just smiled in a highly mysterious way. Then I checked her

tyres and pumped up two of them. She was very grateful. After which I insisted on carrying both her bags into the classroom.

10.50 a.m.
At breaktime I said to her. 'Is there anything you wish?'

She replied. 'You sound more like my genie than my servant.'

We're getting on so well – laughing and joking and everything. As I said to George, 'I'd say Ellen and I are practically going out together.'

12.50 p.m.
This girl, who's supposed to be one of Ellen's best friends, came up to me and said, 'You know Ellen's going out with a boy in Year Eight, don't you?'

I pretended that I did know that and replied, 'My interest in Ellen is strictly professional.'

1.05 p.m.
Told George what I'd just found out. He said, 'I feared she was only toying with you.' Then he patted me on the shoulder and said, 'You do realize Ellen has got a massive scab on her right knee.'

1.35 p.m.
I resumed my servant duties with Ellen –
but in a much frostier manner. I don't like
being toyed with.

3.30 p.m.
The bet in geography felt distinctly half-
hearted today. Afterwards George said,
'We need to come up with something new.
All businesses have to keep diversifying,
otherwise they die.'

Then Jonny came over. George shifted
about uncertainly. I think he's still a bit in
awe of Year Nine pupils. But I feel right at
ease with Jonny now.

'How's it all going, Jonny?' I asked.

'Terrible,' he replied. 'I've got to take
assembly tomorrow, haven't I?'

At first I thought he was messing about.
But he wasn't. He said, 'They're trying to
get you all to play more sport. So I've got
to talk to you about the joys of football
tomorrow.'

'How boring,' I said. Then I added
quickly. 'No offence. I know half the school
are footie-mad.'

'None taken. I don't want to do it, but
I've got no choice.'

'Do you know what you're going to say then?' I asked.

'Haven't a clue,' said Jonny. 'So it could be the world's shortest assembly.'

After he'd gone George said, 'That might make a good bet. How long will Jonny talk in assembly tomorrow?'

I was taken by surprise at first. Up to now we'd only ever gambled on teachers, not fellow pupils. But then I thought, why not . . .? It's just a bit of fun.

WEDNESDAY FEBRUARY 1ST
9.15 a.m.

Assembly today was nothing short of brilliant.

Mr Cummings got up and spoke first. For the rest of the week he said they would be highlighting, in assembly, some sports we might want to get more involved with, starting with football. 'And here,' he said, 'to tell you more about that is a very promising player: Jonny Brooks.'

Jonny was lounging at the front, like a cat reclining in the sun. Beside him was the P.E. teacher beaming around him like a proud parent. Jonny got up and strolled forward. He was carrying a football. 'Greetings, fellow suckers,' he said in that sleepy voice of his. 'This is a football. Look, it's round and bouncy.'

All at once he headed it into the audience. There were gasps and shouts. 'I thought that would wake you all up.' He grinned. 'If you get bored of me you can always play with it. Anyway, I'm supposed to be doing an advert for playing football. So, boys and girls, play football and you can look like me. If that doesn't put you off, nothing will. I love football, actually. It's better than anything else at this place, better than stinking lessons.' Mr Cummings bristled. Jonny laughed to himself as if he'd just made a joke. 'And that's all I've got to say.'

Suddenly the football, which had been bouncing around the assembly, flew towards Mr Cummings. In his haste to escape it, he lost his balance and slipped over. A great cheer rose round the hall now. Jonny gave a little bow. But the P.E. teacher wasn't amused at all and gave everyone the stink eye. Then after helping Mr Cummings to his feet, he made us sit in silence to reflect on our disgraceful behaviour.

But how long had Jonny's talk lasted for? That was the important matter.

George had managed to bring in a stop-watch so we could time it exactly. 'Thirty-five seconds,' he muttered.

The nearest guess was Tyrone, who hissed across to George in a piercing whisper, 'Have I won then?' Afterwards we had to remind Tyrone that the syndicate was an underground organization, and if the teachers got even a whiff of what was going on it would be curtains for all of us. I also pointed out that my sister was just a few rows behind us.

'She might have heard you. And she's definitely an enemy agent.' Luckily she was still buzzing from Jonny's assembly. Well, everyone was.

As I left I saw Mr Cummings talking to Jonny. It didn't exactly look as if he was congratulating him either.

11.00 a.m.
Saw Jonny at breaktime. I told him he should take assembly every day.

'Not much chance of that,' he replied with a wry smile.

'The teachers are only jealous,' I said. 'No one ever enjoys their assemblies.'

'And now Monster has requested the pleasure of my company in five minutes.'

Jonny lowered his voice. 'Heard you had a little flutter on me this morning. Did you win?'

I started with surprise, and then said, 'No, I was way out. I had you down for two minutes, twenty seconds

'Now tomorrow, there's a boy in my class – Vernon West – who'll be delighting you all with a talk on his cricketing career. And he just loves waffling on about himself. Put me down for six minutes, will you?'

Of course the syndicate was closed to new members. George and I had agreed that. So I should have just promised to add his name to the waiting list. But as I pointed out to George afterwards, Jonny was just off to face Monster so this was like his last request. And I couldn't refuse that, could I?

Chapter Seven

THURSDAY FEBRUARY 2ND

9.00 a.m.

A swift change of plan.

Vernon West's talk has been postponed to make way for an emergency assembly. We all groaned when our form teacher told us, because that could mean only one thing: Monster ranting away.

Gloom flooded the classroom until I decided our bet wasn't off after all. No, we'd just switch the gamble to Monster and how long he'd bore us. Well, Chancer forms went whizzing round that classroom.

And I've just seen Jonny and he wants

to be in on the new bet too. Who'd have thought there'd be such a buzz before an assembly with Monster. Feel very proud.

9.35 a.m.
Nothing less than a disaster.

Monster strode in wearing that pin-stripe suit he puts on every single day. He stood for a moment, nose upraised, like a human bloodhound ready to sniff out the tiniest glimmer of mischief. Then he was off, thundering away.

But today's assembly was humming to a new sound. A rebel beat, that only pupils could hear. Today, we had a bet on. Yet no one would have ever guessed. We were sitting there so meekly. But really we'd blown a hole right through school and not one of the teachers had an inkling.

And now we could soar high above the gloom of assembly without moving a muscle. Suddenly I started to smile. I knew I was breaking about fifty school rules but I just couldn't help it. I felt quite giddy with happiness. That's when Monster stopped talking . . . in mid-sentence too. His face was suddenly all twisted with fury. I thought, he's detected me smiling in his assembly. Now I'm in big trouble.

But it wasn't me he was eyeballing so ferociously. It was someone a little further along my row.

It was George.

'On your feet, lad,' said Monster.

George stood up – a crimson, shaking figure. A deathly hush now surrounded him.

'What have you got in your hand?' demanded Monster.

'Nothing,' whispered George miserably, 'except for this stopwatch.'

'Why have you brought that into my assembly?' demanded Monster.

'Because you're being timed, sunshine. And it's a fantastic way to escape from the total tedium of your assemblies without having to move a muscle.'

I'd so loved to have called that out, and if I'd only had twenty minutes left to live I definitely would have done. But instead I just whispered it under my breath, while George struggled to say anything at all. He just released these odd, strangled sounds before Monster squelched him with a stare.

'Do not waste any more of my time,' said Monster. 'Go and wait outside my room now.'

George tottered off and no one knows what's happening to him. Some people are even worried that he will break down and tell all about the syndicate. But I'm not. I know George is made of stronger stuff than that.

But I just hate to think of him facing Monster all on his own. The funny thing is, I was supposed to take charge of the stopwatch today. Only George asked if he could have another go, as he'd enjoyed himself so much yesterday.

9.50 a.m.
Newsflash.
George has just got back. He said he was so scared he thought his head was going to explode. Monster kept him waiting for ages but then just talked to George outside his office. George said, 'He put his face so close up to mine I could count all the blackheads on his nose.' He roared at George for a few minutes, then confiscated his stopwatch, awarded him a double detention and said he'd be calling his parents later.

'Well, it could have been a lot worse. I mean, he hasn't got a clue about the syndicate.'

'Oh no,' agreed George. 'I told him I'd brought in the stopwatch to use in games and he definitely believed that.'

10.45 a.m.
In all the drama I forgot to tell you who won today's bet ... well, actually, it was me. Somewhere inside my head a stadium erupted with a great roar of joy. I was chuffed to bits. Ellen came and congratulated me. But I just said flatly, 'Thanks.' Afterwards I said to George, 'She's missed her chance with me now.'

'I bet she's gutted,' he replied.

4.45 p.m.
After school George's mum and dad were both waiting for him. But George didn't seem as upset as I'd expected. Instead, he said excitedly, 'Look at that. They're actually talking together – and in quite a friendly fashion. Never thought I'd see that again.'

Then he slipped seventy pence into my bag. 'Sorry I can't join you in your time of triumph. Just be sure and enjoy every moment. You deserve it.'

For my prizes I had four ice creams and a wide range of confectionery. Then Jonny rolled up in his effortlessly, cool way. 'How many of those can you eat before you go cross-eyed?' he asked.

'Only about a million,' I said. And then an ice cream dived out of my hand and fell with a mighty splat onto the ground.

'Go on, lick it up, Harvey,' called out a voice. All at once I felt a bit silly.

'I've got to be honest,' said Jonny. 'You've got a quality idea here, but I think your prizes are rubbish. I mean, ice creams are for little kids' parties.'

'What do you suggest then?' asked Lee.

Without a moment's hesitation, Jonny replied, 'I'd tell everyone in the syndicate to put in a pound a day. Then the winner has got a cash prize that he or she can spend on whatever they choose. If they want to buy a load of ice creams they can – but my way, they've got a choice.'

'I think Jonny is right,' said Lee. 'And I'm sure we're all going to get sick of ice creams soon.'

There were murmurs of agreement.

'Well, all your comments are salted away,' I said, tapping my head. 'Let me consult with George and I'll let you know what we decide – thank you all for your participation.'

As he was leaving, Jonny said to me, 'Vernon West's doing his talk in assembly tomorrow. You've got my bet for that already, haven't you?' Then he added, 'I wasn't knocking your basic idea. I think it's brilliant. And I'm chuffed to bits that I've been able to join the Chancer set. The only Year Nine as well.' He looked so happy I couldn't spoil everything by revealing that his membership had only been for the one day.

7.00 p.m.
George managed to sneak a call to me while his parents were outside talking (about him). And he absolutely hates Jonny's idea.

'When you play football or rugby or tennis, you don't have a prize at the end of it. It's the game that's important. Well, it's the same with Chancer, isn't it?' he cried.

'Yeah,' I agreed slowly.

'And the ice creams are just a laugh. They're not meant to be taken seriously,' he said. 'But money prizes will change everything. Take my word for it.' His voice rose. He was getting very worked up.

'I can tell you feel strongly about this,' I said. 'So that's it . . . no cash prizes. I'll tell

Jonny and everyone else tomorrow.'

'Perhaps you'd also tell Jonny he's not in the syndicate any more . . . he'll have to join the waiting list like everyone else. He's just a big show-off really, you know.'

'That's a bit harsh,' I protested.

'No it isn't. Like that assembly he did yesterday. What was all that about?'

'He was just having a laugh,' I said.

'No he wasn't. He was trying to be cool. He spends his whole life doing that. I bet in the evening he practises all his expressions in the mirror for hours. Anyway I think the difference between acting cool and being like a total prat is a very small one.' He added, darkly, 'I'm only glad we copyrighted our ideas so Jonny can't steal them.'

Chapter Eight

FRIDAY FEBRUARY 3RD

9.25 a.m.
Just before assembly I told Jonny what
had been decided by the management (i.e.
George and me) about the money prizes.
And Jonny took defeat very well. I've got
to say that. Then he went on to win today's
little flutter.

A few of the syndicate got a bit cross
about that, saying, 'It wasn't fair.'

I said, 'You're talking rubbish. He won
fair and square, didn't he? Now, stop
moaning or I'll chuck you out of Chancer.'

It's just lucky I have this talent for
stopping crises.

2.00 p.m.
We had an extra gamble today owing to overwhelming public demand. We bet on the number of times Mrs Wadlow, in art, would say 'There's still a conversation going on.' After a slow start she repeated it three times in five minutes and everyone just had a brilliant time.

And the girl who won said to me afterwards, 'School's got such a different vibe now. I can't believe how fantastic it is.'

So George and me have achieved something which many would have said was totally impossible: we've made school fantastic.

5.00 p.m.
After school the whole syndicate – apart from George – went over to the ice-cream van. There were two winners today of course: Jonny and Debbie. Only Jonny started giving all his ice creams and chocolate away.

'Aren't you keeping any of it?' I asked him.

'No, I eat too many sweets anyway,' he replied.

Now if he'd just given away a couple of bars of chocolate, I'd have thought what a generous guy. But to hand it all out – well, he was making a mockery of the whole prize system, wasn't he?

Then Lee piped up, 'This is such a waste. It'd be much better if we had money as prizes. Then we could buy what we wanted . . .' He went on, 'Put your hand up if you'd rather have cash prizes.'

Every single person raised their hand – except Jonny. He said, 'It's not up to us to decide. It's Harvey's syndicate.'

'Thank you,' I said a bit huffily. 'It's mine and George's syndicate actually – and we've made a management decision that we're not messing about with money.'

'So you're just going to ignore our views,' said Lee.

'Not at all,' I replied. 'Your opinions are very important to us.'

'It doesn't look like it,' said Lee. There was rebellion in his eyes now. And not just in his eyes either. Suddenly I was facing a full-scale mutiny. I had to keep my nerve and act fast.

I said I needed to consider their views for a few moments. I went and stood beside the ice-cream van, looking highly thoughtful. But I already knew what I was going to do.

Then I walked slowly back. The atmosphere was suddenly very tense. Jonny came and stood beside me. It was a gesture of support, I think, which I appreciated, even though he was the one who had really started all this.

'Here is my verdict,' I declared. 'Taking into account the strong views of the syndicate, I will allow us to have cash prizes for a trial period of one day only. Each person will give me a pound before the start of school on Monday. Then we will have our normal bet. And the winner will take away all the money in the pot.'

Everyone looked really pleased and excited now. Jonny patted me on the back and whispered, 'Welcome to the big time.'

But I am worried about what George will say. I just hope he'll understand I had to make an emergency executive decision.

SATURDAY FEBRUARY 4TH

5.15 p.m.

I'm totally annoyed.

There I was performing an act of charity when I got shouted at by Claudia.

Mum had asked me if I'd mind returning some books that Claudia had left downstairs. So I carried these books into

Claudia's bedroom, which is much more like an office with a little bed tucked in the corner. There's nothing friendly or relaxed about it at all. Anyway, I was just helpfully putting the books on her desk when she rushed in as if she was being chased by someone.

'How dare you nose about in my bedroom!' she cried. Before I could reply Claudia was yelling 'Mum! Mum!' at the top of her voice. She came charging upstairs, but instead of telling Claudia to stop having a go at me because I'd just been doing a very kind thing, she put an arm around Claudia and said I was to leave immediately.

Favouritism or what!

5.45 p.m.
I stuck this note on Claudia's door. It said:
DO NOT DISTURB – OLD WITCH BEING STROPPY IN HER SMELLY ROOM.

It was only a little joke. That's all. But of course Claudia went mad again. And of course Mum and Dad took her side. Mum told me that I must be more careful how I speak to Claudia and not say things which might start arguments – like 'Hello.'

4.30 p.m.

Just discovered something truly sensational. My head's still reeling. GET READY FOR THE SHOCK OF YOUR LIFE.

Claudia was away, visiting a friend (her only friend Gemma). And Mum and Dad had slipped round to a neighbour's house for half an hour, leaving me home alone.

I decided it was payback time for yesterday. So I marched upstairs and gate-crashed Claudia's room. I thought I'd try and locate this diary there'd been all this fuss about a few days ago. It was probably deeply dull. But suddenly I just wanted to find it. It was like a little challenge I'd set myself.

Well, I searched through all Claudia's drawers and cupboards. But in the end, I discovered it under her mattress.

Only the diary there'd been all this fuss about was blue, while this was a squat, little red one. Yet, on the first page was written: *I shall now start a diary of important events in my life.*

Only Claudia could keep two diaries, I thought. She had to show off at absolutely everything. At first I just flicked through a

80

few pages while standing up. But then I had to sit down and ended up reading every single line.

For this diary was mainly about ... Jonny.

I was as stunned as you are. She gibbered on for pages about his floppy, dark hair, warm, brown eyes and long eyelashes. Then one day he smiled at her (or she thought he did; he was probably just burping or something) and she gushed on about how she felt she'd been missing someone all her life – and it was him.

But next day Jonny ignored her (who could blame him?) and she felt this tide of despair rising over her: *I don't see how Jonny can ever be my boyfriend because when he's near me, I can't even breathe properly*. I immediately pictured her wheezing madly every time Jonny approached and nearly fell off her bed from laughing so much.

Then the diary became even more incredible.

She feared that Mum and Dad were noticing how desolate she felt. And she didn't want them to know her heart was breaking as they think she should pass all her exams before she even thinks about boys. And anyway, they had more than enough to worry about with Harvey!

So the cheeky sausage penned a fake diary in which she pretended she was just worried about her schoolwork. Then she left the fake diary in a very obvious place where she knew Mum would find and read it. After which she pretended to be annoyed . . .

So the diary Mum read was merely a clever decoy. Who'd have thought my sister could be so sneaky? And when Mum and Dad find out the truth . . .

There were some juicy bits in the real diary too . . . well, one bit where she imagined how good a kisser Jonny would be. Dream on, I thought. That's something you will never know.

There was also a bit in her real diary about the time she saw Jonny talking to me. She was dead surprised but supposed Jonny just felt sorry for me!

She went on: *I'm always having to tell Harvey off and put him in his place. He is unbelievably lazy and disorganized and annoying. He must never, ever find out how much I care for Jonny. My blood freezes at the very idea.*

Ha, Ha.

And Ha, Ha, again, but even louder.

I'd always wanted to get something on my, oh so perfect sister and now at last, I had.

But what should I do with this top secret info?'

There was a boy at my old school who found his sister's diary. And in it she wrote about these three boys she loved. Next day he went and told all three boys: 'My sister loves you.' Brilliant crack, that was.

So should I do the same . . . tell Jonny? No, no, I couldn't. Far too embarrassing for him – and me.

I could just swipe the diary and wave it in front of Mum and Dad. But they'd say I had no right taking it and I'd end up in worse trouble than Claudia. Again!

No, I had to store up this knowledge and wait for the right moment . . . then I will strike.

8.30 p.m.

George has finally got his mobile back, but only as an act of charity. His voice was foggy with flu. He thinks he'll be stuck in bed for days. I've promised to keep him posted with all the syndicate news. Only I haven't mentioned the money prizes tomorrow. Of course I will tell him about it – but I thought it'd be better to wait until he was feeling a bit stronger.

9.25 p.m.
All evening I've been smiling at my sister. 'What's the matter with you?' she demanded at last.

'Absolutely nothing,' I replied, then released another smile. I shall wait until exactly the right moment to take my revenge on her. But when I do . . . I just can't wait.

Chapter Nine

MONDAY FEBRUARY 6TH

The alarm shrieks in your ear like a lost banshee. And it's Monday morning. No more depressing time exists, especially if it's wet and cold, which it is every Monday morning.

But today I got up brightly, hopefully. I arrived at school early as well. Only some of the Chancer syndicate members were even earlier. They were waiting for me by the lockers.

'That's what I like to see,' I called out. 'Enthusiasm.'

They had their money all ready. They practically snatched their Chancer forms.

Then a silence fell, heavy with deep thinking. Mr Cummings was taking assembly today. But how long would he ramble on for? His form was variable, so it was a tough one.

'Can I think about this a bit longer?' asked Tyrone.

'Of course you can,' I said. 'I'll accept all bets up to the start of assembly.'

Jonny strolled by. 'This is where it's all happening,' he said, then handed me a pound coin and a stopwatch. 'Keep the watch as long as you like,' he said.

The bell went for the start of school. Jonny declared, 'Ladies and gentlemen, the first game will commence in just fifteen minutes.' Then he gave this little salute and said, 'Be lucky!'

Well, the assembly today was a real nail-biter. You see, bang in the middle of a sentence Mr Cummings spluttered to a halt. Sweat slid down Lee's forehead. Had he won? You could feel the tension in the air as everyone waited expectantly. Lee's legs even started shaking about. I hissed, 'It's like sitting next to a member of *Riverdance.*'

A tiny smile crossed Lee's face. Victory

was so close he could practically smell it. But then, quite unexpectedly, Cummings started gibbering again.

Afterwards Jonny announced, 'If you didn't find that exciting, you're dead.' Felt sorry for Lee, though. It was time he won something.

Joanne, the girl who did win today, is without doubt the quietest member of the syndicate. But as Jonny said, 'That's the great thing about Chancer, it's totally democratic. Anyone can win.'

It has become a bit of a tradition that we all meet up by the ice-cream van after school. So that's where I gave Joanne her winnings. I must admit, having money as a prize added an extra shot of excitement to the proceedings. I took a vote and it was unanimous we carried on with money prizes tomorrow.

I feel we've just naturally graduated from ice cream to money.

TUESDAY FEBRUARY 7TH
1.45 p.m.
This lunchtime, Jonny and me were discussing Chancer business over by the back field. Just to be friendly, I asked him if there was any news about that trial he'd

done for the top football club. I expected him to say 'Yes' and bore me with all the details.

Instead, he cried sharply, 'Now, don't you start. Anyway, I thought you hated football.'

'I do.' I laughed nervously. 'Don't know why I asked you really.'

'Neither do I,' he said snappily. The conversation went a bit dead then, until he suddenly asked me, 'Can you keep a secret?'

'Keeping secrets is one of my specialities,' I replied. 'Why?'

Jonny didn't answer, just motioned me to follow him. We slipped through that gap in the fence, which led into the totally-out-of-bounds woods. We sat under the oak tree exactly where I'd met with George a couple of weeks ago.

'The club did ring up,' muttered Jonny quickly. 'And they've turned me down.'

I was astounded. The whole school was waiting for Jonny to be signed up.

'I got my chance,' said Jonny flatly, 'and I messed up. There were thirty of us at the trial and they said ninety per cent of us wouldn't make it. After that my head was just all over the place.' He shook his head.

'And I was rubbish.' He started pulling up some grass. 'It's my dad I feel sorry for. He started me off playing football in the park. I owe him everything . . .'

'What did he say?' I asked.

'Nothing. I think he's still in a state of shock. He's hardly talking to anyone. Gone right into his shell.'

Faraway, the bell went. Jonny got up. 'Not a word, all right, Harvey.'

He looked so serious, I mumbled, 'I won't let you down.'

Jonny's face relaxed into his usual grin. 'Now, let's get back to important matters like . . . Chancer.'

Only last night George had rung demanding to know if Jonny was out of the syndicate yet. But Jonny's got enough problems in his life without chucking him out of Chancer as well. So I've decided Jonny's a member for life, if he wants.

And George will just have to accept that.

7.45 p.m.

I've found out who's taking assemblies for the rest of the week. Thought I'd put this info in a special Chancer newsletter. I was working away on this when I spotted Dad in the doorway. I quickly covered up what

I was writing. Dad said, 'I didn't mean to disturb you.'

'That's all right.'

'You're really getting stuck into that homework, aren't you?'

I smiled modestly. 'It has to be done, so you may as well give it your best shot.'

'Well, keep up the good work,' said Dad.

'I intend to,' I replied, immediately returning to the Chancer newsletter.

8.45 p.m.
And here it is.

LICENSE TO GAMBLE ©

Official Newsletter   issue 1

INSIDE

We reveal WHO is taking this week's assembly

PLUS!! *Nose Blowing: Latest results AND very detailed drawings!!!*

BE LUCKY!!

9.20 a.m.

The newsletters are a big success. Now people really feel they are part of an elite group. In registration some of the syndicate have brought in lucky mascots. I saw Lee furiously rubbing this rabbit's foot. And ever since Jonny said 'Be lucky!' this has become our special password. Just before we went into assembly everyone was hissing 'Be lucky!' to each other and doing the salute as well.

I tell you, a little flutter kicks the day off to such a brilliant start.

And after assembly, if you've got a boring lesson (and let's face it, most of them are boring) it really doesn't matter, as you need some time to relax after all that excitement.

5.30 p.m.

I was resting on my bed, reflecting on another superb day, when my sister burst in. 'Tell me it isn't true?' she wailed.

'It isn't true. Now clear off,' I said, briskly.

But her next words went through me like a knife. 'You're running some sort of awful gambling club, aren't you?'

Shocks like that are really bad for your

health. And for a few moments all I could do was make these strange, gurgling noises.

'And please don't give me any of your silly lies,' said Claudia. Then I saw she was waving something in her hand. One of the Chancer newsletters. 'Gemma found this in the bin.'

'Trust her to be nosing about in bins,' I muttered.

'She thought it was something I should know about.'

'I bet she did,' I murmured.

'And Gemma told me you gamble for money. Is this true?'

'Well, you see—'

'Yes or no,' she snapped.

'At this very moment, yes – but the prizes we offer are constantly changing. And it's not as bad as you think. We just have friendly little bets on things like the number of times a teacher might blow his nose in a lesson.'

'Oh honestly, haven't you got anything better to do with your time?' asked Claudia in this really scornful tone.

'Actually, Claudia, it's highly educational. It makes us observe people and there's a skill to it as well.'

She shook her head. 'What total rubbish!'

'Look, it's just a harmless way for pupils to relax. It gives them a break from all their pressures. It's a new therapy for schoolchildren, really.'

Claudia started making loud scoffing noises.

'Honestly, Claudia, you're witnessing the start of something big here. Don't ruin it, please.'

She raised her eyes. 'Have you lost every brain cell?'

'Probably,' I grinned at her.

Not a flicker of a smile back. 'Let me tell you something,' she declared, 'gambling in school is illegal and pathetic. I didn't expect this, even of you. And it must stop tonight.'

'Tonight?' I echoed disbelievingly.

'You will text all your fellow gamblers and say it's over. All gambling stops immediately. If you don't, I shall have no choice but to inform our parents about your behaviour.'

'Look, just—'

'No, Harvey, you may as well save your breath and get texting now, as there's absolutely nothing you could say

94

that will change my mind.'

With that she sailed out.

Everything was going so superbly. And now I am facing the biggest crisis in my entire life.

More than anything I want to keep Chancer going.

But how can I?

I've got to think about this.

Back soon.

5.35 p.m.

Back already. The shock must have made my mind go blank. How could I have forgotten that I held a trump card? Claudia's diary. I'll do a trade with her: my silence if she does nothing about the syndicate. And I'll do it right now.

5.38 p.m.

Haven't gone yet because I think I've got an even better plan.

5.40 p.m.

'Be lucky!'

That's just me writing it to myself. The whole future of Chancer rests upon what happens next.

7.25 p.m.

Just returned from Claudia's room where I put my plan into immediate action. As soon as she saw me she demanded, 'So have you told everyone? Have you closed it?'

'Not quite—' I began.

'I don't believe it,' she interrupted. 'You leave me no choice.'

She was actually on her way to blab to Mum and Dad when I cried out, 'There's just one thing I thought you'd care to know. In the syndicate is a boy from Year Nine . . . Jonny.'

This stopped her in her tracks all right. Gemma obviously hadn't found that out. She turned round and looked at me.

'I'd say he's just about our keenest member,' I went on. 'And he and I have become mates. Well, you've seen us hanging about together. We talk about everything. No subject is out of bounds – not even you.'

She immediately looked away and asked in this funny, muffled voice, 'What exactly have you two been saying about me?'

'Oh, Jonny's dead curious about you. Full of questions.' I was lying my head off now. He hadn't asked one thing about her.

'I said to him, why don't you just go off and talk to Claudia yourself. She's isn't that scary. But he just went all shy and said he couldn't.'

Suddenly I remembered something from that sloppy diary of hers. 'He told me how he sees you across the playground and wants to smile and say hello but somehow never does.'

Claudia's breathing rate was definitely on the increase now. 'But why can't he come and say hello?' she asked.

'Because you're so far above him – intellectually. That's what makes him all nervous.' Then I added, very casually, 'By the way, are you interested in him at all? He asked me yesterday, but I said I wasn't at all sure.'

Claudia gave a little gasp as if she'd just touched something very hot, then she half-fell on to the edge of her bed.

I continued, 'What you need, I suppose, is some kind of go-between. I could do that for you, if you want. Funnily enough, we have most of our chats about you when he's placing his bet with me.' I paused here, my heart thumping like crazy. And she didn't say anything for several moments. She just sat staring intently at the carpet while her ears had turned bright red.

Then she said, without looking up, 'I just cannot approve of gambling. No good will ever come of it. And if you don't text your friends tonight, I shall have no choice but to tell Mum and Dad.' She did add, a bit more softly: 'I'm sorry.'

So that was it. I was defeated. I left without another word. And I was just about to pick up my pen and tell you the crushing news when Claudia appeared in my room again.

'I do realize,' she said, 'that it's not easy to dismantle something you've put time into organizing... so I'm giving you until Friday to close things down.'

This was something. So I murmured 'Thank you' in a very polite voice.

Suddenly she was looking right at me. 'And tell Jonny not to be afraid to—' Her voice gave a little crack. 'Well, he can say hello to me any time he wants.'

'He'll be so happy when I tell him that,' I said. 'In fact, it'll make his day, his week.'

She actually blushed before rushing out. PHEW!

Chancer is safe . . . very temporarily.

But of course Jonny isn't really

interested in my sister. Why would he be? She's a total minger with a ghastly personality. No boy on earth would want to spend time with her.

And as soon as she realizes Jonny isn't interested in her ... that's the end of everything. So somehow, I'll just have to string her along. That won't be easy though ...

Suddenly my life is just brimming with problems.

Chapter Ten

THURSDAY FEBRUARY 9TH

8.45 a.m.

Before collecting the bets this morning – both for the Mayor's assembly and for the nose-blowing in geography - I announced. 'Someone here has put us in grave danger.' At once everyone started looking at everyone else. 'Someone left their top-secret newsletter hanging about yesterday. Do you have any idea what could have happened if a teacher had found it? Or what about Monster?'

I paused here to let my powerful words sink in. 'Well, I don't think any teachers did see it, this time.' I never mentioned my sister. I thought it would be best if I kept that a private matter. 'But next time . . . well there mustn't be a next time.' There were murmurs of agreement. 'OK, warning over, eyes down now for another day's gambling.'

After everyone had placed their bets Ellen came back. 'The person who left that newsletter hanging about... well, I think it might have been me.' Her eyes turned down in shame. 'I really thought I'd tucked it safely away in my bag, but later I couldn't find it.' Her voice sank to a whisper. 'It's been on my mind ever since.'

'Well, thanks for coming and telling me,' I said, sounding a bit like a teacher. 'And you won't make that mistake again, will you?'

'I really won't,' she cried.

'So let's just forget it now.'

'Thanks,' she whispered.

'And, be lucky.'

She looked up; a tiny smile crossed her face. 'Be lucky, Harvey.'

She sounded a bit as if she meant it as well.

11.05 a.m.

Jonny won again today. His eyes lit up like car headlights when he found out. And he still looked extremely pleased with himself at breaktime. So I thought this might be a good time to ask him to smile at my sister. Only I couldn't just blurt it out like that. I had to be deeply subtle.

So I asked him, 'Are you up for another little bet. A private one?'

He grinned. 'Go on then.'

'I warn you; this will take a great deal of nerve. It concerns Claudia, my sister.'

'Funny, I never think of her as your sister,' said Jonny.

'I try and not think about it either. All I want you to do is go up to her and talk to her for thirty seconds. And oh yes, while you're talking, show her all your teeth as well.'

'That's a weird dare,' said Jonny. 'What's it all about?'

'I regret I can answer no questions at this stage,' I said. 'I just need to know if you accept the challenge.'

'Oh, I accept it all right,' said Jonny. 'What's the prize?'

'Another pound if you complete your task, a pound to me if you fail.'

We shook hands and then Jonny found Claudia. I was watching the proceedings from a safe distance, with a stopwatch.

And yes, he talked to her for a full thirty-four seconds. And he was flashing those smiles about too.

I handed over the pound to him. He asked, 'Any other girls you want me to talk to?'

'Not right now,' I said, 'but well done. You endured my sister for over half a minute.'

4.15 p.m.
Claudia's just dropped into my bedroom. 'Actually, Jonny talked to me today,' she said lightly.

'I told him to have a bash.'

'He asked about maths homework,' she went on.

'Well, that's because you're so intellectual.'

'I told him it wasn't an easy homework but I'd be pleased to help him.' Her voice gave a little shake here. 'He didn't answer me though, just went off again.'

'That's because of the strength of his feelings,' I replied. 'They just totally overcame him.'

'Did they?' she gasped.

'Oh yes – you have a very powerful effect on him, you know. But don't worry, I'll keep

on telling him not to be so shy around you.
You just leave it all to me.'

She actually thanked me for my help
before she left!

FRIDAY FEBRUARY 10TH
4.00 p.m.

At the start of school I was by the lockers
collecting people's money for today's
assembly bet. I was pretending to bite the
coins to check they weren't chocolate – and
there was such a good feeling in the air.
You'd never have guessed we were at
school.

Then suddenly I realized we were being
watched by the caretaker. He's what you
might call a lurker, always on the lookout
for trouble. He loves catching you out and
reporting you to one of the teachers. He
came rushing over to us, his straggly
moustache bristling excitedly. 'Now, what's
going on here?' he demanded, pointing at
me. 'Why are they all giving you money?' I
had to display some quick thinking.

'They're only lending it to me.' I blurted
out. 'You see there's this new CD player I
really want, but I'm broke so a few of my
very kind mates here clubbed together . . .'
I gabbled on for ages like that. By the way,

here's a useful tip for you: if ever someone catches you doing something you shouldn't, make your explanation very long and very boring. They'll usually let you off just to shut you up.

That's exactly what happened here. In the end the caretaker raised a bony hand and said brusquely, 'All right, I've heard enough. But be careful. Money can get stolen.'

'That's something I'd never thought of before,' I replied.

After school, by the ice-cream van, Jonny declared, 'We can't let teachers see us handing Harvey money again. They'll definitely get suspicious next time.'

He proposed that everyone gave me a fiver for the week's gambling on Monday. While this transaction was taking place, two Chancer members would act as guards checking no teachers were roaming nearby. The money would then be kept securely in my locker until Friday afternoon, when I doled out all the week's winnings.

Immediately afterwards Jonny asked for a vote. Everyone agreed his idea was an excellent one. So did I, actually. It was just – well no one especially asked for my opinion. It was as if I were just an ordinary member – not the co-executive director and co-total controller of Chancer ©.

4.30 p.m.
My sister's just burst into my bedroom again. She wanted 'a little chat'. I thought she was going to ask if I'd closed the syndicate (which of course I haven't). Instead, she wanted to know if Jonny had given me a message for her. There was a dead hopeful look on her face. So I thought I'd better say something.

'Well yeah, he did actually. I should have told you before. He said . . .' I paused and could feel her looking at me really intently now; ready to feast on every word. 'He said he hopes you have a top weekend.'

A belting message there, I thought. Only she didn't. I could tell right away. No, she wanted something yuckier. Now, I don't really do yucky. But amazingly, I came up with a killer line today. 'Oh yes, he also said to tell you he'll be thinking about you a lot this weekend.'

That hit the spot all right. Now she was blushing as red as a traffic light. 'Are you all right?' I asked.

She nodded, but she looked as if she was about to burst into tears. Had I overdone it? I didn't want her getting too carried away with joy, especially as Jonny had not actually said a single word of the garbage I'd just spouted.

So I added, hastily, 'Of course he'll be busy playing football and training and stuff, so he won't be thinking about you all that much. I think what he meant is that he'll try and squeeze in the odd thought about you now and again.'

But I was talking to myself. She'd gone into a kind of trance. She walked out of my bedroom like a sleepwalker.

I tell you, my sister gets weirder by the hour.

SATURDAY FEBRUARY 11TH

Claudia's still drifting about in a dream. And she hasn't mentioned me closing the syndicate once. I think I might have got away with that one – for now, anyhow.

SUNDAY FEBRUARY 12TH

George rang – and in quite good spirits. 'Dad's been round to see me every day this week and he and Mum haven't shouted at each other at all. That's a good sign, isn't it?' I agreed that it was. 'I was getting so sick of them rowing all the time . . . I just want them to behave properly again.'

Then he told me he was back at school tomorrow. So I couldn't put it off anymore. I had to fill him in on the changes to Chancer. He listened to me in total silence, which was a bit eerie. Once I even asked him if he was still there.

'Well, say something,' I cried. 'I feel as if I'm talking to a ghost.'

'And I feel a bit like a ghost,' said George. 'I've only been away five days and yet so much has happened . . . why can't things just stay the same, especially when they're good. And Chancer was just perfect as it was . . . perfect.'

George sounded really upset. What could I say to him? In the end I cried in this fake, cheery voice: 'Never a dull moment with Chancer. It keeps you on your toes all right, I can tell you. That's why I'm glad to have my co-director back with me.'

'So let me get this straight. It's just cash prizes now – and nothing else?' He sounded flat and disappointed, as if I'd somehow let him down.

'Yeah, just cash prizes,' I said, quickly.

'That's what everyone wanted. I was only responding to changing demand – all businesses have to do that, don't they?'

I waited hopefully for him to agree. Instead, he asked, 'And what about the servant option?'

'We seem to have dropped that,' I replied.

'That's a pity,' he murmured, 'a huge pity. These changes were forced on you by Jonny, I suppose.'

'Of course they weren't,' I said, a bit annoyed.

'And you haven't made him co-director or anything?'

'Now you're just being silly,' I said.

'I just thought I'd better check,' said George. 'Well thank you for this useful update.' His words might have sounded friendly enough. But his voice was like thin ice cracking.

I just hope when George comes back tomorrow, he'll see that I haven't been disloyal to him in any way. And all the changes were very necessary.

9.30 a.m.

Another syndicate has started up in Year Seven. And it's an exact copy of Chancer. Jonny found out about it. He immediately confronted the organizers. Told them the Chancer syndicate is copyrighted, all rights reserved – which means it can't be copied without our complete permission. Jonny said he was also charging them a pound a week each for using our ideas. 'Just call it a little bit of VAT,' he said.

George went ballistic when he found out what Jonny had done. He said no one should ever have to pay us money. We weren't running some sort of protection racket. He also said Jonny had no right to make decisions like that. It was up to the co-executive directors, no one else. He got so worked up, he was soon gasping for breath.

Anyway, I backed George up. I didn't like the idea of pupils paying us money either. It just seemed dodgy somehow. Jonny said he was only trying to help and he thought we could have put the copyright money into an emergency fund for expenses. But he fully accepted our management decision.

10.45 a.m.
George and me have decided the new syndicate can continue operating. But we have the right to inspect their records and close them down if we're not happy. We're also meeting them on the back field this lunchtime for a quick training course. This was George's idea. He said it's to ensure quality control.

1.35 p.m.
Just finished our first Chancer training course. I let George take charge, so he's looking as pleased as punch now.

Afterwards I said to him, 'This morning I actually saw pupils going to school laughing – you're more likely to spot a unicorn frolicking about than a sight like that. But it's happening here. And do you know what Tyrone said to me at breaktime today? '*As soon as assembly starts I can feel this electricity running through my veins.*' No pupil in the history of the world has ever said that about assemblies before . . . we should both feel very proud and not fall out over little details.'

I thought George might say switching to cash prizes wasn't a little detail. But instead he said, solemnly, 'I agree with you. Thanks to our invention, no pupil in this school need ever be bored again. That's an incredible achievement.'

TUESDAY FEBRUARY 14TH

Jonny said to me, 'Your sister keeps thanking me for my messages. Haven't a clue what she's on about. But I've got the strangest feeling you have.'

'Funnily enough, I do. Look, will you just go along with what she says and if you can bear it, flash her the odd smile as well. She's going through a very stressful time at the moment . . . so just keep on humouring her, will you?'

'You sound very concerned about her,' said Jonny.

'Oh I am,' I replied gravely.

Jonny burst out laughing. 'Oh yeah, I really do believe you . . .'

'Well, just look on it as a favour to me,' I said.

Still grinning, Jonny asked, 'When will you tell me what this is really about?'

'Soon,' I replied. 'But for now, think of it as your good deed for the day.'

4 p.m.
Thinking of Jonny and Claudia and

suddenly remembered what day it was! So I've been forced to do something truly awful: buy a Valentine's Day card. Claudia will definitely be expecting one from Jonny. So I got this gruesome one with a massive heart on. I lowered my head so the assistant wouldn't recognize me.

Later I whispered to Claudia, 'A card's just arrived for you. I've left it up in your bedroom.'

I've never seen her move so fast

WEDNESDAY FEBRUARY 15TH

Rumours are flying about that Jonny's now had offers from a number of football clubs and is busy sorting through them all.

'My dad's put that out,' said Jonny. 'Total rubbish, of course. But I'm playing in the under-fifteen team the weekend after next, and Dad's really hoping some scouts might be watching. Yesterday he bought me this new kit. But I made him take it all back. I said if I turn up wearing brand new stuff everyone there will hate me.'

THURSDAY FEBRUARY 16TH

You won't believe this. Maybe the Valentine's Day card was a mistake. Claudia's been all moony ever since and tonight she told me she needed to talk to Jonny properly and couldn't at school. So she wanted me to invite him here over half term next week. Then I could breeze off and leave them to really get to know each other.

I thought she had a nerve actually. I mean, he's asked her about maths homework, and he's been smiling at her all week. What more did she want? Some people are just never satisfied.

I said to her, 'Well you know how hard Jonny finds it talking to you, because of all these feelings fizzing up inside him.'

'I do realize that,' said Claudia quietly. 'But I think it's time for us to be decisive. Maybe I should just ring or text him.'

'I like your style,' I said. 'But I really think it might be better if I invited him here and he comes across you casually.'

She thought about this. 'Yes, I can see that,' she said slowly. She looked up. 'I never thought you and I would be sitting here talking about this.'

'It's come as a bit of a shock to me too,' I replied.

FRIDAY FEBRUARY 17TH

Gave out all the winnings for the week after school, by the ice-cream van. 'I'm rich,' cried Tyrone, running about waving his money.

Then I asked Jonny if he'd like to come over to my house during half term. Claudia had suggested next Thursday afternoon, as Mum and Dad would both be out then. He agreed at once. Later I told Claudia. She had to take several deep breaths.

Chapter Eleven

SUNDAY FEBRUARY 19TH

HALF TERM

George has left to stay with his dad for a few days. He was allowed to pay me a quick visit first. Of course we spent the whole time talking about Chancer.

MONDAY FEBRUARY 20TH

Here's a sentence I never thought I'd write. At nine o'clock this morning, I found myself MISSING ASSEMBLY.

TUESDAY FEBRUARY 21ST

Claudia's already started going over the arrangements for Thursday. She said,

'When Jonny arrives I'll let him settle first.'

Let him settle! He wasn't a pigeon.

'Then I'll just casually appear in the doorway and ask if he'd like a cup of tea or coffee. After which, you'll bring him downstairs and then leave us together in the kitchen.'

A very funny look came into her eyes after she'd said this. And it bothered me. I didn't want her suddenly trying to kiss Jonny or something. I couldn't put him through that torture. So I said hastily, 'Last time I spoke to Jonny he said he wasn't feeling so well.'

'Oh dear,' she twittered, all concerned.

'Yeah, he thinks he might have a touch of flu. Well, you know how infectious that is. So I wouldn't get too close. Just have a quick chat across the kitchen table.'

I hope that's warned her off.

WEDNESDAY FEBRUARY 22ND

My sister's always saying: 'Oh, I can't be bothered how I look.' This is pretty obvious when you see her. But today she's been into town to have her hair done (a slight improvement, I suppose).

She told Mum and Dad she just felt like

a change. They don't know anything about Jonny coming round tomorrow. In fact, she hasn't even told Gemma.

THURSDAY FEBRUARY 23RD

2.55 p.m.
Jonny's due round any minute. I can hear Claudia in her bedroom chanting 'I'm calm, I'm calm' over and over, while I'm getting more and more apprehensive.

A full report soon.

5.15 p.m.
What an afternoon!

Jonny arrived just after three o'clock. He was wearing a battered T-shirt and grey pinstripe trousers. He prowled around my bedroom looking at all my posters and admiring my new CD player, which my occasionally generous parents had given me for Christmas. I was starting to enjoy myself when Claudia burst in. She was all dressed up – even wearing a bit of lipstick and eyeliner – but acting highly surprised to see Jonny.

'Oh, I'm sorry, Harvey, I didn't know you had a friend round.' She was talking dead slowly, just as they do on those tapes for people learning to speak English. And her right hand was shaking quite a lot.

'Jonny, you know my sister Claudia, of course.'

'Of course,' said Jonny, giving her one of his vast grins.

Now both her hands were shaking. 'I'm just making a drink. Would you care for tea or coffee?' she asked.

'No, I'm all right, thanks,' said Jonny. This wasn't what he was expected to say. Claudia could only stare at him with her mouth half open. She looked like a mechanical toy whose batteries have just run out.

'Well, I'd really like a coffee,' I said. 'Are you sure you don't want something, Jonny?'

'Definitely,' he said firmly.

A few minutes later Claudia called upstairs in this high, shaky voice, 'Your coffee's ready, Harvey.'

I got up and then said to Jonny, 'You come along too . . . you can see our kitchen.'

'And that's something I've always wanted to do,' grinned Jonny.

Downstairs, Claudia was hovering by the kitchen door like a waitress waiting for a tip. Then she started flicking her hair about in such a desperate way I nearly burst out laughing. Anyone would think she was about to do something vitally important – not just chat to a boy in the kitchen.

I picked up my mug of coffee and disappeared. Felt bad just abandoning my mate like that – but Claudia really hadn't left me any choice. Now I know exactly how people who are being blackmailed feel.

I hovered about for an entire four and a half minutes. When I returned they were talking about football. Claudia's as uninterested as I am – but she was pretending to be all fascinated. And she was nodding her head at Jonny like one of those nodding dogs you see at the back of cars.

Back upstairs Jonny asked, 'So what happened to you?'

'I got lost,' I replied.

He looked at me. 'You're not trying to set me up with your sister, by any chance?'

'I'd never do anything so gross,' I replied, indignantly.

'Come on, something's going on here,' he said.

I decided it was time to come clean. I

told him everything – even about the gruesome Valentine's Day card - and ended by saying, 'So you're the price of my sister's silence.'

'*Me?* But I thought she'd go for someone intelligent.'

'It doesn't look like it,' I grinned.

He pretended to hit me, then said, 'I'd never thought I'd be her type.'

'Stop complaining. I'm not any girl's type.'

'Aaah,' he cried.

'No, I'm pleased. I couldn't bear to have a girl wasting my time . . . but going back to my sister, you don't have to do anything stupid with her like kissing. But could you just act as if you like her a bit. I know it's a massive amount to ask . . .'

'No, I can do that all right,' said Jonny. Then he added, 'As it happens, I wanted to ask you a little favour as well.'

'Just name it,' I said at once.

'Well you'd better hear it first. It's an idea for the syndicate, actually.'

'OK,' I said a little more cautiously.

'How about one extra flutter a week? Ten pounds each.'

'Ten pounds!' I gasped.

Jonny's voice rose enthusiastically. 'We'd call it the connoisseurs' bet and it would be strictly voluntary, as some people won't want to bet all that. And that's cool. I know it'll take that extra bit of bravery . . . so that's why it's just for the connoisseurs. But Harvey, just picture the tension and excitement . . . it'll be like going on the Wheel of Death at the fair. And the scariest rides are always the best, aren't they? So what do you say?' Before I could reply Claudia started humming very loudly downstairs, reminding us she was still around.

'Shall I say a few more words to her?' asked Jonny.

'If you can stand it.'

'Oh, no sweat . . . so how about the connoisseurs' bet, Harvey? Will you give it a go? There's so much tension in my house at the moment with another football trial this weekend . . . knowing I had something to look forward to would help relax me. It might even make me play that little bit better. You never know.'

He was smiling his familiar, teasing grin. But I could sense how much he wanted this. Meanwhile my sister hummed on . . .

'All right,' I said. 'But just as a one-off though.'

'I know I'm going to play superbly now,' said Jonny. And he practically charged downstairs to talk to my sister.

Yes, I do know I should have consulted George before agreeing to Jonny's request. You don't need to remind me. But he wasn't around. So I had to make another executive decision.

And it will just be a one-off bet.

Chapter Twelve

This is me starting to get up to my neck in it.

(this is 'it'!)

FRIDAY FEBRUARY 24TH

5.30 p.m.

There's a great vase of flowers in Claudia's room now. I asked her where they had come from. 'Oh, I couldn't resist buying them, they looked so beautiful,' she said breathlessly. Then she was off asking me some more stupid questions about Jonny and what he'd said about her.

Thinking up yukky stuff is really hard work, you know. I'm dead exhausted from it all.

SATURDAY FEBRUARY 25TH

6.30 p.m.

George is back. He called me almost immediately.

He wasn't in a great mood. His parents have returned to their bad old ways. 'All week Dad and Nan were making snide comments about Mum and trying to find out things. And now Mum's started asking me all these questions about Dad . . . while I'm just stuck in the middle. I think I'd rather be raised by wolves.'

This really wasn't the best time to tell him about the connoisseurs' bet. And it would have been better face to face, rather than on the phone. But I wanted to get it over with.

When I told him Jonny had come round on Thursday he was immediately suspicious. 'I was expecting something like this. A special meeting, was it?'

'It wasn't a meeting at all.'

'But you did discuss Chancer,' he persisted.

'It came up in conversation. Yes.'

'I just knew it would,' said George with a gloating relish.

'And he had an idea . . .'

'What a surprise.'

'If you'd just let me speak, instead of keep interrupting with sarky comments I could explain it to you.'

'I can't wait,' he murmured.

But he did listen to me in silence about the connoisseurs' bet – well, he gasped once or twice, but that was all.

'So what do you think?' I asked, not at all hopefully.

'I think it's a freakishly poor idea.'

'Any particular reason?'

'It's far too much money for a start. Some people will be wiped out if they lose. Of course, you never take any notice of me. If Jonny told you to have a connoisseurs' bet every day, you'd do it.'

'That's so not true,' I cried.

'Prove it then, by saying no to this grisly idea. Ring him now and tell him it's our syndicate – not his.' Then he slammed the phone down.

6.50 p.m.
I am having second and third thoughts about the connoisseurs' bet now. Should I, at least, postpone it?

7.15 p.m.
Claudia's just whizzed into my room

whispering how Jonny's sent her a text message, asking if she wants to go to the cinema with him next Saturday. So Jonny's volunteering to spend a whole evening with my sister just for the sake of Chancer. That's beyond brave.

And for performing such an act of reckless courage Jonny surely deserves a small reward. So the connoisseurs' bet really must go ahead after all. That will please Jonny. But I'm calling it an experiment – and no further connoisseurs' bets can take place without the complete support of both members of the executive. I hope this will please George.

SUNDAY FEBRUARY 26TH
5.45 p.m.
Actually, it didn't please George at all. And he's just sent me this horrible e-mail. It says:

Dear Harvey,
This is to inform you that I am resigning from co-management of the syndicate. I have viewed recent events with alarm and view this most recent event with even greater alarm. I have grave misgivings about the future of Chancer, and cannot

127

continue in my present managerial capacity. My resignation takes effect from the moment you read this.

My decision is final and definite.

Yours, highly regretfully,

George.

PS. As you know, I have kept a record of all the bets – and winners. I shall let you have this notebook tomorrow, as it is of no further interest to me.

I have already e-mailed him back:

Dear George,

Your resignation is not accepted and never will be. My decision is also final and definite.

Harvey.

6.15 p.m.
George's reply, to my reply:

Dear Harvey

Actually, there is no need for me to esign – my job just doesn't exist any more. You and Jonny are running the syndicate now – and soon it'll be just Jonny in charge.

We were a great team. But not any more.

There is no point in texting me or ringing me again, as I have nothing more to say on this matter to you.
George.

My reply to his reply:

We've invented the greatest improvement to school life ever – and now you're going off in a mood. I hope you will come to your senses by tomorrow. Chancer is bigger than your dislike of Jonny. You remain co-executive director and co-total controller.
Your mate, always,
Harvey.

7.15 p.m.
Quick phone call from Jonny. He says he thinks the football trial went better than last time, but now the waiting starts. Then he asked me if we were still on for the connoisseurs' bet. I reminded him it was just an experiment. 'Oh sure, sure,' he said airily. 'But it's going to blow a hole right through school.'

MONDAY FEBRUARY 27TH
Arrived a bit late at school today. When I got there, discovered Jonny had already

told the syndicate about the connoisseurs' bet tomorrow. He said everyone was up for it – with the exception of one girl and George. And he'd already found replacements for them – two boys from Year Nine.

I was just standing there, blinking, as I was told all this. I hate arguing with people – and I didn't want to dampen Jonny's enthusiasm – but some time soon, I'm going to have to remind him who's running Chancer.

On my desk in the classroom was George's notebook, listing all the bets so far. I said, 'So you haven't changed your mind?'

'I'm more certain than ever.' He looked both hurt and angry. There was so much else I wanted to say. The words hung in the air, waiting to be said. But in the end I just walked away from him.

Cheered up a bit in assembly. The air crackled with excitement and the atmosphere lifted me right out of my troubles. That's the great thing about Chancer. The not so great thing is that Chancer is currently the cause of all my troubles.

This evening I made out some special

connoisseurs' bet cards and a list of things
to do tomorrow:

1. Collect in all the money for the
connoisseurs' bet.
2. After the bet, announce there will not be
any further connoisseurs' bets until both
executives agree on this.
3. Tell George what is happening and try
and persuade him to resume his executive
position.
4. Kindly, but firmly, remind Jonny that
while he is a highly valued member who
will be committing an act of reckless
bravery on Saturday night for which we
are all very grateful, he is not in charge of
the syndicate.

TUESDAY FEBRUARY 28TH
9.05 a.m.
I'd collected in the entire connoisseurs'
money (one hundred and twenty pounds)
by the start of registration. And I had
already been given a fiver by everyone
yesterday, too, with a jackpot class bet
to replace today's connoisseurs' bet so
there were lots of chances to win. But
the big prize would be won today. My
form room was just bubbling with

tension. One hundred and twenty pounds – all resting on just one assembly. That's a very substantial amount. You could go on holiday for that.

After the end of registration Lee jumped up and turned round in a circle. He said he was trying to change his luck.

Then Ellen sat down again with a heavy sigh. 'Are you all right?' I asked. I feel I have to take a friendly interest in all my members.

She said, 'I always get a little tingly before a bet but today . . . I just can't go in, Harvey. I'm too worked up.' She'd turned deathly pale as well.

But I took charge of the situation.

'You'll be as right as rain in a second,' I said. 'Just take a few deep breaths . . . go on, do it now. No one else is watching.'

She took five deep breaths, then got to her feet and thanked me for my swift action.

Jonny was standing outside the assembly hall with the other two Year Nine boys who'd joined our syndicate for this one time. 'Here we go,' said Jonny, grinning at me. Even he looked keyed up.

'Have you kept my old stopwatch in good working order?' he asked.

'I polished it this morning,' I grinned.

Then he gave me that funny, little salute and cried, 'Be lucky!'

9.25 a.m.

GAMBLING IN ASSEMBLY – An exclusive eye-witness report by Harvey.

Make no mistake. This was the big one. The buzz along my row was incredible. People couldn't have been more excited if they'd been at a cup final. The assembly hall had blossomed into a casino, without any of the teachers realizing.

Then Mr Cummings trudged forward. He only has to appear for your eyes to feel heavy. But today his first word (it was also his second and third) – 'Erm' – was like a pistol shot.

We were off.

The odd word about uniform filtered through to us. But of course we were living in two worlds now: the dreary, everyday one and the fantastic Chancer one.

And in the Chancer world our skin tingled, our pulses raced . . . while poor Ellen was soon practising her deep breathing again. The minutes just flashed past . . . eleven, twelve . . . Cummings must stop soon. 'Keep going for just a bit longer,' I muttered. 'Go on, you can do it.'

And it really looked as if I might win. Cummings was spluttering to a halt at thirteen minutes . . . exactly what I'd bet. Suddenly Ellen wasn't the only one doing some deep breathing. But then he raised a hand to read out a notice. That notice cost me victory. He went on for another thirty-eight seconds, which meant Jonny had pipped me at the post.

Outside, Jonny turned a somersault. Then he let out a cheer which rang round the school. But he announced he'd wait until Friday to receive his winnings with everyone else. 'It'll give me time to decide how I'm going to spend it.'

He was triumphant and everyone was pleased for him.

9.35 a.m.
No, they weren't. I wanted everyone to be pleased for Jonny. That's why I ended my report like that. After all, that's the sporting way. But to be honest, the air was thick with jealousy (to be absolutely honest, I had a few twinges myself).

The syndicate (apart from Jonny) slunk out of assembly, looking so miserable you'd have thought they'd just left double maths. And that wasn't the aim of Chancer at all. It was supposed to raise people's spirits – not add to the grimness of school life.

Lee and another girl started moaning that they'd never once won. Jonny heard them and said, 'What you've got to do is act as if that bet never happened. Just forget it and think about tomorrow's bet and the day after that, because one time you will win.'

'That's easy for you to say,' they muttered.

1.30 p.m.
I'm totally astounded. A few minutes ago Jonny asked me if we could have another connoisseurs' bet tomorrow!

'What are you talking about?' I cried. 'We're all broke now.'

'I can draft in a whole new group of volunteers easily.' As he said this I noticed a gang of Year Nine boys hovering nearby.

'No, I'm sorry Jonny – not tomorrow. Can't afford it.'

'Go on mate, I'll lend you what you need. You nearly won today. So tomorrow you could be rich. Think of all the lovely money.'

I hesitated.

He went on, 'We're hitting the big time now, Harvey, so you've just got to go with it.'

I glanced around at those Year Nine boys circling round us. And I felt surrounded, trapped. So I said firmly, 'No Jonny, we can't have any connoisseurs' bets tomorrow. It's just too soon. That is my executive decision... but well done again on winning today.'

'All right,' said Jonny in a soft, low voice. Then he gave me what I can only describe as a chilly glare. And it shocked me, because it was so different from his usual laid back manner.

Later I saw him going for a moody walk on his own. He didn't let on that he saw me.

So, in less than forty-eight hours, I've managed to fall out with both George and Jonny. I can hardly bring myself to think about that. So I won't.

WEDNESDAY MARCH 1ST

4.30 p.m.

I didn't particularly enjoy the bet in assembly today. Maybe it was because I had no chance of winning (my bet was way off). Or it might have been because Jonny was in such a frosty mood. I'd never seen him like that before.

But I'm standing firm on the connoisseurs' bets issue. I told George this today. Only he was too busy sulking to listen properly.

Life is very tense right now.

Chapter Thirteen

THURSDAY MARCH 2ND

8.35 a.m.

Something terrible has just happened.

Arrived at school to see the door to my locker swinging open. I feared the worst and I was right. My locker had been broken into and all the money for this week's syndicate (sixty pounds plus one hundred and twenty for the connoisseurs' syndicate, making a grand total of one hundred and eighty pounds) had gone.

I'd bought a top of the range lock as well. Never believed anyone could get through that. But they have. And now I can't think properly. Too riddled with shock.

What a way to start the day. I never ever expected to see that. Still, I am a leader so I must just somehow stay calm – and work out what to do now. I suppose the first thing is to hold an emergency meeting of the syndicate.

9.00 a.m.
I said, 'Members, prepare yourselves for a massive shock,' then paused, to allow them to do exactly that, before announcing, 'I regret to inform you, the syndicate has been hit by a robbery... all of this week's prize money has in fact been stolen.' Everyone boggled at me in total consternation.

'As you know, I'd bought a deluxe lock which I thought was impregnable, yet someone found a way of breaking into it.'

'But who?' asked Ellen.

Several names were immediately suggested. Then I declared, in a masterful voice, 'They may have taken our money but they can't rob us of our spirit. I say we go ahead with the bet today.' Everyone agreed. There were a few cheers. Jonny – his irritable mood having completely slipped away – even patted me on the back. And I felt kind of heroic.

Then I announced that I had a plan to cover the cost of all the stolen money if the thief weren't found, to the sound of more cheers. But actually I didn't know what I was talking about. I just got totally carried away there.

10.50 a.m.
Jonny, Lee and me have just finished a search of all the Year Seven lockers. It was completely voluntary and no one refused. I never really expected to find the money just sitting there. Yet I thought we might discover a significant clue. Only we didn't.

Then Lee suggested everyone in the syndicate be searched – just so they could be ruled out of the investigation. I did this (and insisted Jonny search me). Everyone was clean, as I'd expected.

'What do we do now?' asked Ellen. 'Go round and search the rest of the school?'

'We can't do anything which will attract the teachers' attention,' said Jonny. 'Let's go back to the scene of the crime. The robber must have left one clue.'

We did this, but were still clueless when the bell went.

12.45 p.m.

I've just spoken to George.

'I hate to say I told you so,' he began.

'Well don't say it then,' I snapped.

'Is it true you're going to cover the cost of the stolen money?'

'It is,' I replied, a little shakily.

George frowned. 'When you made the special connoisseurs' bets forms and with big money involved, you should have put at the bottom: *The Management cannot accept any responsibility for the loss of your money. You enter completely at your own risk.* Car parks do that, you know.'

'Oh, do they?' I asked.

'You must have seen those notices stuck up, saying if your car or any valuables get pinched, don't expect any help from us. You're completely on your own.'

'That's a bit harsh,' I said.

He sighed. 'No it's not, it's business. Keeping all that money in your locker was just asking for trouble.'

'I had a top of the range lock and ... well, I never really thought any pupil would steal from the syndicate, as we're on the same side as them.'

George shook his head. 'You can be so innocent, Harvey.' Then he said quietly,

'Just by chance I was at school earlier than usual this morning.'

I pounced on that piece of information. 'Did you see anyone acting suspiciously?'

'Yes I did,' he replied, in the solemn tones of someone giving evidence in court. 'You're not going to like this, but facts are facts ... I saw Jonny loitering about by the lockers.'

'So what,' I replied at once. 'That doesn't prove anything.'

'If you say so,' murmured George.

'And anyway, most of that money was Jonny's winnings. So why would he go to all the trouble of stealing it when he'll get the lot on Friday anyhow?'

'I'm only telling you what I saw,' said George stiffly. 'He's not usually at school that early, is he?'

'Neither are you,' I said.

'Right, fine,' said George angrily. 'I'm obviously wasting my time. I just hope you can sort this out.'

2.30 p.m.
Sitting in French doing some maths. Money owing to syndicate – one hundred and eighty pounds.

Money in my pocket – twelve pounds,

sixty pence.

Money still owing to the syndicate – one hundred and sixty-seven pounds, forty pence.

WHAT SHOULD I DO?

1) Go bankrupt – I could do this but only as a very last resort.
2) Be a servant to those whose money has been stolen. I'd then be a servant for about the next three years.
3) Sell something. My most valuable possessions are (in order)
   a) My CD player
   b) My fart machine
   c) My guitar

If I cannot unmask the thief I shall have no choice but to sell the three possessions as listed above. One problem there: how do I sell my CD player without my parents noticing and asking questions? (They probably wouldn't miss my fart machine or guitar.)

Another problem: I'd miss my CD player very much.

Can heads explode from thinking too much? Well, I think mine is about to do just that. I feel worn out and full of despair. But I don't think anyone would guess as I'm hiding it exceptionally well.

4.45 p.m.
Now I am totally and completely confused.

After school, I was chatting to Jonny. I was telling him how I planned to sell some stuff.

'You shouldn't have to do that,' he said.

'Got no choice,' I replied. 'The money was in my keeping . . . so I am responsible.'

He looked at me. 'I tell you what, I'll buy that CD player from you if you like. Mine's packing up anyway. That'll totally wipe out your debt with me.'

'I don't think it's worth a hundred and twenty pounds.'

'So what.' He waved a hand dismissively. 'That'll do for me. But one problem, it leaves you without any music.'

'I've got a radio.'

'No, you want your own music. It's not right to deprive any human being of that.' Then, out of absolutely nowhere he said, 'There's only one thing for it. We'll have to stage a robbery in your house.'

'A robbery,' I repeated, as if the word was a ball we were bouncing back and forth to each other.

'We just make it look as if somebody's

broken into your house and nicked your CD player. That way your parents buy you a new one and you've paid off a load of your debt as well – so whichever way you look at it, you're laughing. Now when's a good time to break in?'

I grinned. 'Tomorrow afternoon would be perfect as Claudia's playing in some concert at the Town Hall, which my mum and dad just can't miss . . .'

But I was only messing about. You know how you plan mad things with your mates. And you spend ages working it all out but you know you'll never really do it, don't you?

So that's what I thought Jonny and me were doing, just having a laugh together.

Only then Jonny suddenly muttered, 'Try and skive off last lesson, that'll give us a bit more time.' And he said it so seriously, just as if we were actually doing it.

Now as you know, I'm the King of the Dares. I'll do anything that's a bit daft. But making it look as if my house has been robbed, I'd never do that.

Far too warped for a start. And well – it just doesn't feel right.

Surely Jonny realizes that.

6.15 p.m.

Thought I'd better ring up Jonny to sort out this little misunderstanding. He was rushing off to football training so it was only a brief chat.

He asked me, 'Is your sister still up for the cinema on Saturday?'

'Is she still up for it?' I cried. 'It's merely the highlight of her entire life. In fact, she's probably counting down the hours as we're speaking. Of course you know what she's looking forward to the most?'

'Amaze me.'

'You giving her a great, big sloppy kiss.'

He nearly killed himself laughing then. We both did. And he never even mentioned the fake burglary. So I didn't either. I'd obviously been panicking unnecessarily. It was all just a big joke. I really should have realized that. Sometimes I can be so unsophisticated.

Chapter Fourteen

FRIDAY MARCH 3RD

9.20 a.m.
No sign of Jonny at school today. I'm sort of relieved.

11.00 a.m.
George has just handed me an envelope. 'What's this?' I asked.

'Your fighting fund,' he said. 'I've been collecting for you.'

I was a bit embarrassed. 'I don't feel as if I should take it. I'm not a charity case.'

'You take it,' said George, pressing it into my hand. 'They've been enjoying the benefits of the syndicate, it's only fair they should dip into their pockets when there's a crisis.'

'All right, you've persuaded me. How much is in there?'

'Fifteen pounds,' he replied.

I was impressed – and sort of touched as well. After the morning's bet, the boy who'd won kept on asking me when exactly he'd receive his prize money. I had replied, 'Expect your winnings shortly. It's all in hand.' But I didn't like his attitude one bit. So George's collection cheered me up no end. Only there were no coins in the envelope, just three five-pound notes. That's when I guessed this money had come from just one donor: George. But he was already walking away from me. I called after him, 'Thanks a million for this. But why don't you un-resign from your management role? The syndicate really needs you.'

George didn't reply, just shook his head a little sadly.

Want to hear something shocking? For a moment there I actually envied George and wished I could resign from the syndicate too. Sometimes the responsibility is just so heavy – well it gets me down, if you really want to know the truth.

I suppose I'm experiencing what people call the pressures of high office.

1.25 p.m.
Newsflash
Jonny's just popped out of nowhere. He hissed, 'Meet me outside the school at three o'clock sharp.' His tone was very crisp and businesslike.

'So we're definitely on then, are we?' I asked.

He looked astonished by my question. 'Of course we are. So don't be late . . . and, you haven't seen me, all right?'

Then he was gone again.

All at once everything felt so weird and unreal – like one of those mad dreams.

And I don't know what to do. I suppose I could just not turn up at three o'clock. That's what George would say to do.

But I can't let Jonny down. And that's not because I'm afraid of him or in his power or anything daft like that. But I do care what he thinks of me. And if I bottle out... no, I'll just have to go through with it. Anyway, Jonny sounds as if he knows what he's doing. Dead organized.

And I'm only going to burgle my house

very slightly. See how I'm talking myself into it.

So it looks as if the next time you hear from me I shall have robbed – myself.

6.00 p.m.

HOW TO ROB YOUR OWN HOUSE HARVEY'S STEP-BY-STEP GUIDE

THINGS TO DO

1. Pick the right time.
This must be when all your family are out and there aren't too many neighbours sticking their noses in, either. That afternoon was very dark and very gloomy. In fact, the sky was so low it seemed to be tumbling down on to the tops of the big trees. So absolutely perfect weather for robbing yourself.

2. Disguise yourself.
This was Jonny's idea. He bought me a football scarf and a hat. Then if any neighbours happened to glance out of their window they wouldn't immediately recognize me. There is no need to get carried away with disguising yourself though.

False beards, for instance, are not really vital.

3. Bring the right equipment.
Black gloves and a small hammer are all you really need. Jonny and me went round to the back of the house. Jonny smashed the glass by the door handle of the conservatory with his hammer. The key was still in the lock, so in just a few seconds he had turned the lock and we were inside the conservatory – and the door leading into the kitchen was open already.

'It's dead lucky it's us breaking in – and not a proper burglar,' said Jonny.

I agreed it was. I even told myself I was teaching my family a valuable lesson about home security. So I was doing them a favour really.

4. Be considerate.
I swept up all the smashed glass. Also, Jonny and me both took our shoes off. I doubt if true burglars would show such good manners. But Mum was going to be upset enough by the break-in. No point in having mud on the carpets as well.

5. Relax.

I found this very difficult, especially when we first broke in and there was this gloomy silence, apart from the rain spitting on the window. I just felt as if I shouldn't be there, which is pretty mad when you think I was in my own house.

Jonny kept telling me to: 'Stop looking so tense.' To relax me, he related this story about how he won his first ever cup in a penalty shoot-out competition. 'The tiniest cup you ever saw,' he said. 'But I was so scared of burglars nipping in to steal it, I used to keep it under my bed every night.' That did make me smile – briefly.

6. Make the robbery look as authentic as possible.

Jonny said it was a bit unlikely that a burglar would break in and just take my CD player (even though it is quite superb). We had to make it appear as if they were going to take loads more stuff – until they got disturbed.

So we opened all the cupboards, strewing stuff about (Jonny said the two things burglars mainly search for are money and jewellery) and I think it looked highly authentic.

THINGS NOT TO DO

1. Have a blazing row with your fellow burglar.

Jonny placed my CD player into a large carrier bag with the words: 'Get in there, you beauty.' He was in such a good mood now. He said, 'On Monday, Harvey, you can tell everyone I've been paid back in full – that'll impress them all right – and they'll be next. Then it's business as usual with the ordinary syndicate, and how about a special connoisseurs' bet on Monday too?'

'I'm sorry, Jonny,' I said firmly, 'but it's a definite and total no to that. The connoisseurs' bet is just for very special occasions.'

'Well, make Monday a very special occasion,' said Jonny with a crafty grin.

'No, I'm afraid I've made a management decision on this matter.'

'But you can un-make it,' he cried. 'Come on . . .

I shook my head.

He stared at me wildly. 'If it's looking after the money you're worried about, let me do that. I'll take full responsibility.'

I replied. 'No, it's not just that. Look, Jonny, I've still got a load of money to pay back.'

He immediately dug into his pockets. 'I can lend you some money – how much do you need – twenty, thirty . . . ?'

Suddenly all this cash was just flowing out of his wallet. 'Take what you need,' said Jonny. 'Go on, have it all if you want.' He was practically pleading with me to take it. Why?

Ever since George had told me he'd seen Jonny hanging about by my locker I'd had this tiny, little suspicion – and it was no more than that – that Jonny might have stolen money from my locker and got himself a free CD player as well. I never really believed that, though. But the suspicion wouldn't quite go away. It floated around the edge of my mind like smoke.

All at once it just flared up inside me. But I was only thinking it in the privacy of my brain. Yet it must somehow have burst through my eyes as Jonny cried, 'Why are you looking at me like that?'

'Like what?'

'You think this is the stolen money, don't you?'

'No, no, not really . . .' I spluttered.

'Not really!' he yelled.

'Not at all,' I hastily corrected myself. 'It's just someone saw you hanging about by the lockers on the morning when the crime happened.'

'Who?' he demanded.

'That doesn't matter.'

'I bet it was George . . . I should punch you in the face for even thinking—' he began.

And then something else happened.

THINGS NOT TO DO (continued)

2. Forget to leave the scene of the crime
Jonny and I were arguing at the top of our voices when a car pulled up. That panicked us all right and reminded us what we were doing there. Jonny spluttered, 'They mustn't see me here – and certainly not with this.' He picked up the bag containing *his* CD player.

I told him to go and hide in the back garden and I'd let him know when he could make a getaway. He was rushing off when he slipped and fell. He lay sprawled out on the carpet. I rushed over but he quickly scrambled to his feet and hissed, 'If ever you need my help again, don't hesitate to get lost.'

The second he left, the key turned in the lock. I sprang forward. I wanted to prepare my family for what they were about to see. 'Hello, everyone,' I cried. 'Hope you all enjoyed the concert. Now, please don't be shocked, but when I came home – just a few minutes ago – I discovered two men in the house. They were robbing us actually. It was just lucky I arrived home before they'd really got stuck in. And when they saw me they scarpered. I chased after them but they moved like lightning . . .'

I stopped here for breath. Mum, Dad and Claudia were staring at me in utter consternation. I had been speaking pretty quickly.

'So we've had burglars?' squeaked Mum.

'I'm afraid so,' I said.

'But how did they get in?' asked Dad.

'That I don't know,' I said.

'But are you all right?' cried Mum, putting an arm round me. 'That's the important thing.'

'Oh, I'm as fit as a fiddle – just wish I'd been able to catch one or both of them for you . . . that's my great regret.'

THINGS NOT TO DO (continued)

3. Feel guilty

Much, much harder to avoid than you might think.

Every time your parents are nice to you, your skin starts crawling and you feel as if you've just swallowed something very cold. I even started shivering. Can you believe that? You must try your hardest not to copy my shameful behaviour.

Dad soon worked out how 'they' had got in, while Claudia went stumbling about all the rooms, giving little reports as she went. 'They've emptied lots of drawers but they don't appear to have taken anything.'

Then she called me upstairs to my bedroom. A grave-faced Claudia informed me. 'I think they've stolen your CD player.'

I'd prepared myself for this scene and immediately let out a huge sigh. 'How I shall miss that old CD player,' I said in a small, broken voice. 'Well, it wasn't even that old . . . it was pretty new, actually.'

She nodded and looked so grief-stricken I had to turn away and open my wardrobe door. 'Oh well, at least they haven't nicked my rather fine fart machine.'

Claudia didn't answer. I think she was too moved by my bravery. She did put an arm around my shoulder though.

Never in my whole life have I been hugged as much as I have tonight.

9.30 p.m.
It was ages before I could escape into the back garden to check up on Jonny. The air was cold and smelled of rain. I took a few, large gulps. I felt as if I'd been trapped inside my house for weeks. And I couldn't find Jonny. I've rung him a few times but he's not answering either. So now I've left him a message. I just said: 'Thanks for all your top help. Give me a ring as soon as it is convenient.' I was a bit over-polite actually. That was to cover up my great embarrassment.

Mum and Dad have said they'll buy me a new CD player. So I suppose this operation has been a total success. Yet that is not how it appears to me.

Robbing your own house is a weird experience and it also sends your stress levels soaring. So it definitely shouldn't be attempted by anyone with a weak heart. *Warning:* It may also leave you with pangs of severe guilt.

Chapter Fifteen

KABOOOOOM!

↑ The Sound of my world falling apart

SATURDAY MARCH 4TH

9.30 a.m.

Mum brought me a cup of tea in bed. She mentioned Dad might be contacting the police about 'our break-in'. I nearly spilled the tea all over myself.

'Don't look so concerned, love,' said Mum. 'You've nothing to worry about.' Then she smiled at me in a highly affectionate way.

It's a pity my parents only seem to like me when I'm chasing away burglars.

9.45 a.m.

Dad's out talking to the neighbours,

asking if they saw anything suspicious yesterday afternoon.

I'm not bothered about a new CD player now. Honestly. I just don't want my parents to find out the truth. I'm thinking of them as well as me. Well, sort of.

11.00 a.m.
Dad returned from his investigation with a dead thoughtful expression on his face. I tried to appear nonchalant, which is extremely tiring when you're feeling exactly the opposite.

2.30 p.m.
Mum's just left for a conference. She'll be away for a week and wasn't sure if she should still go. But Dad insisted. 'Don't worry, I'll look after everything here, just as I'd promised,' he said. He's driving her to the conference. So they're both away right now.

Just before Mum left, though, she gave me a very odd look. I keep thinking about it. She was just so different to how she'd been this morning. I also heard her whispering to Dad and him saying, 'Let me handle this my way, please.'

What do you think is going on?

Still haven't been able to talk to Jonny. I know he was at football training today. But I'm surprised he hasn't given me a quick call.

5.00 p.m.
Claudia's been discussing tonight with me. 'Dad's due home about half past six. The same time as Jonny is picking me up for the cinema. Now Dad's just had one colossal shock with the burglary – so I think I should spare him another one right now. That's why I rang Jonny saying I'd call for him.'

'You spoke to Jonny?' I said.

'No, he was at football practice, so his mother answered. She sounds lovely.'

But was Jonny still intending to go with Claudia to the cinema tonight? I really wasn't sure. Thinking I should prepare Claudia I said, 'I just hope that when Jonny sees you his feelings don't overpower him so much he has to . . . cancel.'

'Now stop worrying,' she trilled. 'I'm seeing you in a new light these days. You're really quite a caring person, aren't you?'

I gulped. 'Yes, that's me all right.'

5.45 p.m.
Claudia's just left. She put this dress on and then asked me what I thought. 'I like it,' I said. 'But then I've got terrible taste.' She'd done the very best with herself, I've got to give her that. She'd washed her hair and everything.

I just hope Jonny doesn't bottle it now. He's only got to sit next to her in the cinema for a couple of hours. He hasn't got to hold her hand or anything revolting like that. And it'll be dark most of the time, so he won't even have to look at her very much.

I know Jonny's narked with me but this is for something greater than him and me – the syndicate.

No, Jonny won't let me down.

6.15 p.m.
Dad's rung. He's staying to have something to eat with Mum, so he won't be back until after nine o'clock now. I told him Claudia was visiting Gemma but I was absolutely fine on my own.

6.30 p.m.
Claudia will be hitting Jonny's house now. I've just had this little rumble of anxiety

about her. I'm worrying about my sister! What kind of freak am I turning into?

7.15 p.m.
Claudia's back, already!!

She charged up the stairs and slammed her door in a real I-want-to-be-left-alone way.

This is terrible.

Jonny's obviously told her to get lost and she's none too pleased about that. I'll have to go and talk to her. I'll be very understanding as well and . . . got to stop, because my bedroom door is opening.

7.35 p.m.
This week's been littered with horrible shocks. But now I've just had the worst one of the lot.

When my bedroom door opened it was, of course, my sister. And she had a little smile on her face. Then she said, 'I've got the most marvellous news for you.' Her voice was very soft but her eyes were big and staring. I somehow knew great danger lurked.

She went on, still with that crazy, little smile on her face. 'I'm delighted to tell you, Harvey, I've just found your CD player.'

'Why, that's wonderful news, Claudia,' I cried, my voice shaking all over the place. 'Wherever did you find it?'

'It was so funny. I called round to see Jonny, only he still wasn't back from football training and his parents were entertaining some friends so I said I'd wait upstairs in his bedroom for him. And guess what was the very first thing I spotted?' She paused and looked at me, her eyes growing wilder every second. 'A CD player, which looked so very familiar. So when his mum brought me in a cup of tea I asked her about it. And she told me Jonny had only bought it yesterday – second-hand from a friend. But of course, we know better, don't we?'

I could only gape at Claudia. And what made it even worse, she was still smiling at me. Only now her smile matched her eyes. It was positively demented. She cried, 'You gave Jonny that CD player as a bribe to go out with me. Then you tried to pretend it had been stolen so that you could get another one. I have to say, it was quite an ingenious scheme really.'

I struggled to speak but she raised an imperious hand. 'Don't even try and deny it. I couldn't bear it.' Suddenly her voice started to wobble. 'Have you any idea how degraded I feel. The only way a boy will take me out is if you give him a CD player. Am I so awful?'

'Oh yes,' I said, at once, then quickly corrected myself. 'I mean, no, I've seen girls who are worse looking than you and I bet there are ones with worse personalities too.'

'Thank you so much.' She spat the words at me. 'Of course Jonny's only been pretending to like me – just so I won't tell about your precious gambling syndicate. You've both behaved absolutely despicably.' Then she marched out.

I rushed after her and called out. 'Jonny might have bought my CD player from someone in the street.'

She whirled round. 'Is that the best you can do?'

'For the moment, yes,' I admitted.

'Well, I wonder what Dad will think of your suggestion. It's time he knew your CD player has turned up. He will be so pleased. And he should be back soon—'

'No, Claudia, please don't.'

'Why ever not?' she demanded.

Before I could reply there came three loud knocks on the door. It made us both jump. I opened the door. Claudia was just behind me. It was Jonny. He looked straight past me to Claudia. 'Sorry I was out when you called. Would you believe our coach broke down on the way home, but we can still make it. I'll ring for a taxi.'

'I've changed now,' replied Claudia flatly (actually, she hadn't). 'And anyway, there's no need for this farce to continue. I know everything. I'll leave your fellow-conspirator here to fill you in on all the gory details.' Then she tore upstairs and slammed her bedroom door again.

I half-whispered. 'Claudia found my CD player in your bedroom. She thinks that was a bribe to make you go out with her. Talk about a mess. What do you think I should do now?'

'Start praying,' replied Jonny coldly. 'By the way, I'm returning this to you.' He jammed his Chancer membership card into my hand. I wasn't expecting that at all. My legs even went a bit wobbly with the shock. When I looked up, he'd gone.

Nothing is turning out the way I'd supposed. Every hour, my life just gets more complicated.

7.55 p.m.

Thought I ought to try and talk to my sister. She was sitting downstairs in the dark staring at the television. But she wasn't really watching it. She seemed a million miles away.

I called out suddenly, 'Jonny didn't take that CD player as a bribe. No, some money got stolen out of my locker and most of it was money Jonny had won, fair and square. So I gave him my CD player instead of . . .'

'I'm sorry,' she said wearily. 'But you've mistaken me for someone who's remotely interested in what you have to say. All I know is you have ruined my entire life.'

That was a bit of a shock. 'Well, I'm very sorry about that . . .' I began.

'Will you just stay away from me. Do you think you can manage that?'

'Yes, I think so.'

'And will you start by leaving now?'

'If that is your wish,' I said.

'My wish is never to have to see you again, but I don't suppose that would be possible. But you can at least stop talking to me.'

I fled without another word.

9.55 p.m.

They say even the darkest cloud has a silver lining. Well, here's my silver lining: Claudia didn't squeal on me to Dad. Never said a word. So that's good news, I suppose. But I will not hide my true feelings from you. Right now I feel just as if a really dense, thick fog has come down over me. And I'm totally and completely lost in the middle of it.

SUNDAY MARCH 5TH

5.00 p.m.

Atmosphere is just terrible. Claudia's walking around looking like a dead codfish and totally ignoring me. I'm the invisible man today, all right.

And Dad's looking tired and fed up too. A few minutes ago he asked me if there was anything else I wanted to tell him about the burglary. I've got a horrible feeling he suspects something. But Dad won't start shouting or anything. That is not his way. He thinks he's a modern dad. So he'll be more subtle and just wait for me to crack and confess all.

7.15 p.m.

I've come to a major decision. Get ready

for a huge shock.

I've been sitting here dreading school tomorrow. And the reason had nothing to do with teachers and lessons and everything to do with the syndicate. I hated the thought of another week of it. All the fun and enthusiasm had leeched out of it. Now it was just like an awful job I was stuck with.

And then a thought fell on me like a ton of bricks. Why had I got to keep on running the syndicate? It wasn't really my job at all. I was a totally free agent.

Just realizing that cheered me up considerably.

And now I have done something else: I've texted a very important message to all members of the syndicate.

Here's what it said:

Greetings fellow members...

Grave news, I'm afraid. I have reluctantly but definitely decided to disband the syndicate. I realize this will be a heavy blow and apologize for any inconvenience it may cause you now and in the future.

But the burden of this syndicate has just proved too much. And it's stopped being a laugh, which was the whole point of it anyway.

Please keep your Chancer membership cards in a safe but secret place. If ever I decide to start up Chancer again, your membership cards will still be valid. But don't get your hopes up.

Right now I am totally sick of it.

I shall end by thanking you for the good times and saying, for the last time ever: Be lucky.

Harvey, (co-founder and currently in sole charge of Chancer)

PS. All money owing to members will be paid very shortly. You have my word on that.

Chapter Sixteen

MONDAY MARCH 6TH

10.45 a.m.

Shock and amazement everywhere. No one can believe I've closed the syndicate. Everyone's been moaning at me. Tyrone demanded, 'How are we going to put up with school now?'

And yes, I'll come clean: I do feel as if I've let everyone down. Still, it would have been nice if just one person had come up and said, 'Harvey, I wanted to thank you for making school so enjoyable.' It wouldn't have killed someone to say that – and it'd have made me feel a whole lot better.

There's also a storm brewing with that

alternative Chancer syndicate. They just can't agree on the rules or who's in charge. And now there's been a massive row. They wanted me to sort it out, but I just said, 'It's not my problem any more. Sorry.' More stunned faces.

Then at breaktime I got an ear bashing from George. 'You never even consulted me, just went ahead and closed Chancer down without a word—'

'You'd resigned,' I interrupted. 'Or have you forgotten that little fact?'

'Actually, I was considering my position,' he said.

'Well how was I to know that?'

He frowned hard. 'We were making history with our invention and now you've dismantled it all.'

'All right,' I said. 'You start the syndicate up again. Only this time you can run it while I consider my position.'

'Now you're just being daft,' said George. Then he muttered something else.

'What was that?' I demanded.

'I merely expressed an opinion.'

'Well express it a bit louder.'

George said in a low voice. 'You made a fatal mistake allowing Jonny into Chancer. That was when it all started going wrong. You totally ignored my warnings on this matter.'

'You blame everything on Jonny,' I said. 'You even think he stole the money – a charge he totally denies, by the way.'

Suddenly George reddened. I stared at him.

'You did really see him hanging about by the lockers?' I said.

'Yes, of course,' said George quickly. But his face was even redder.

'You little liar,' I cried, shocked and amazed. 'You made it all up, didn't you?

George didn't answer.

'Come on, at least admit it.'

'I just wanted him out of Chancer,' whispered George. 'He ruined everything with his connoisseurs' bets and all that rubbish. I was so weary of him.'

'I'm really disappointed in you,' I cried. 'I never thought you'd do something like that.'

'Well, now you know,' said George and walked off.

1.15 p.m.
I wanted to apologize to Jonny for half believing that libellous slur on his character. But he was not at school today.

173

I was going to leave a message on his mobile. But then I decided that was a bit cowardly. I will wait until he returns to school and deliver my apology face to face.

4.05 p.m.
Something really odd has just occurred. George's mum has rung up wanting to talk to me. (That's not the really odd thing, although that was a shock for a start.) Then she asked if I would return to school immediately. When I asked why, she replied, 'Well George has climbed a tree at school and is refusing to come down again.'

That's not a sentence you hear very often and I repeated it aloud to check I hadn't misheard – and I hadn't. 'If anyone can get George to come down, it's you,' she said. George's mum flinging compliments my way. Odder and odder.

She obviously didn't know George and I had quarrelled today. Still, I bet I can get him to come down. But just why is he stuck up a tree anyhow?

Dad's home early and has offered to drive me back to school.

More soon.

5.45 p.m.

I thought I knew exactly which tree George had climbed – and I was right. It was the large oak in the little woods just past the back field. He was sitting almost at the top, very still, as if he were posing for a picture or something.

At the bottom of the tree was his mum, Mr Cummings and Monster, who was shouting at George through a megaphone. 'You must come down now,' he yelled, as if George was a criminal caught in the middle of a jailbreak. 'You have no right to be up there. You're on private property.'

But it was as if sound couldn't travel up that tree. George never moved a muscle. He just went on roosting up there.

Then George's mum spotted Dad and me speeding towards them. She cried out, 'Look, George, here's Harvey,' as if I just happened to be strolling along the back field at this moment.

Dad and me crawled through the gap in the fence. 'He just won't come down!' his mum wailed. 'What are we going to do?' She looked very upset.

'How about' – I quipped – 'sticking a fifty-pound note under the tree. That should get him down.' But actually, someone only needed to talk to George, nice and quietly. And that someone was me.

So I suggested everyone else back away and I'd swarm up and have a chat with George. Monster didn't like this idea at all. He called me over to him. His eyes were as dead as a shark's. Just looking at him makes you want to shiver for a very long time.

'What do you know about this?' he hissed.

George's mum replied for me. 'I fear this is all George's own idea,' she said firmly.

Monster turned to my Dad. 'Are you allowing your son to climb this tree?' Dad confirmed that he was. 'All right then,' said Monster doubtfully. 'Your father is taking full responsibility for your action.'

So I started climbing. Every so often there'd be this great burst of wind and all the branches would begin swaying about. Once I nearly lost my balance. There was a gasp from George's mum. I gave her a cheery wave so she knew all was well.

When I reached George he was still staring out across the wood, as if it was the most fascinating sight he'd ever seen.

'Hi, George,' I said, trying to be normal. 'Fancy meeting you up here. How are you doing?'

He didn't answer.

'You're not going to ignore me, are you?' I cried indignantly. 'After I've sweated my way up this tree as well. You could at least say hello.'

George slowly turned round. 'Hello,' he said. His face was as grey as the sky above him.

'George, is there any special reason you're up this tree now?'

'I like it up here.'

'And that's cool . . . but there's not a lot to do up here, is there?' I said. 'I suppose you could throw things down at Monster.'

'It's peaceful.'

'Not right now it isn't. Got a right circus going on down there,' I cried.

'They'll get bored and go away,' said George.

'They won't you know. But why have you chosen this particular moment to go tree-climbing?'

George replied in this dazed, faraway kind of voice. 'I don't want to go home. I don't want to go anywhere. So I thought I'd sit up here instead.' Then he snapped,

'And if you've come up here for an apology, you're wasting your time.'

'It's not me you should be apologizing to.'

'No, it's wonderful Jonny, isn't it. Well I'll never apologize to him.' His branch shook in horror at the very idea. 'He spoiled everything. It was all going so well. You were having such great ideas too. I mean, when you had that servants-for-a-day idea, the hairs on my arms stood up. That's how good it was. But then you threw it all away and now it's over. Finished. The end.'

'Its not the end of us being good mates,' I said, a bit shyly. 'That'll last for as long as we live.'

George shifted about a bit then.

'And you've got to remember what we achieved.' I lowered my voice. 'For weeks we ran a syndicate which massively improved pupils' lives. And we were never discovered. Just think about that, George: we ran a highly illegal operation – right under Monster's nose too. I mean, look at him down there, thinks he's Spiderman and . . . the Wicked Witch of the West, all rolled into one. But he hasn't a clue what we've been doing in his school, has he?'

I grinned and suddenly George's mouth flew open and he released this great howl of laughter. Soon he was laughing so vigorously I was afraid he might fall out of the tree.

'All right, control yourself,' I hissed, while tears of laughter started falling down my face too.

Then I heard Monster yell. 'You must come down, George. We have been very patient – up to now. Do you hear?'

George didn't reply. He was still shaking with mad, hysterical laughter. I whispered, 'Listen, if you don't come down now they'll call the fire brigade or the RAF or something and they'll just carry you down like a lost kitten.'

That stopped his laughing fit all right.

'But I've got one of my little plans.' I whispered it to him and after he'd nodded, I scrambled down the tree again.

'George has agreed to come down,' I said, 'but only after you've agreed to his demands. Over to you, George.'

Then he yelled down, 'First of all, Mum, you've got to stop picking me up from school. You only do it to spy on me. Secondly, you must allow me to see my mate Harvey whenever I wish. Thirdly, you must stop saying bad things about Dad. Fourthly, Dad must stop saying nasty stuff about you. I need to know you agree to my conditions before taking one step downwards.'

'Yes, I agree. Of course I do,' said his mum in a strange husky voice. She looked greatly stirred by George's words. So, actually, did my dad. Mr Cummings looked as if he just wanted to go home for his tea while Monster was busy yelling at George through a megaphone again. 'Nothing will be said about your behaviour this time. But remember, you are on private property, so you must take care not to damage the tree in any way.'

Slowly George climbed down the tree. When he reached the ground he gave me a quick grin. His mum rushed over and put her arms around him, then stepped back and looked at George as if he'd been away for months.

Back in the car Dad was full of questions about what had happened. I was surprised by his keen interest. Since the fake burglary the atmosphere between us had been distinctly strained. I was sure Dad was waiting for me to confess everything. But suddenly he and I were all friendly again. Dead weird.

8.15 p.m.
George has rung. He sounded absolutely shattered. He's just had very long chats with his mum and (by phone) with his dad. They've both promised to pull their socks up and greatly improve their behaviour. So, a result there.

TUESDAY MARCH 7TH

10.45 a.m.
I've just apologized to Jonny. He listened to me in complete silence then said quietly, 'When you accused me of breaking into your locker—'

'I didn't exactly accuse you,' I interrupted.

'Yes you did,' said Jonny firmly. 'And I was so angry. I thought, he's supposed to be my mate and he doesn't know the first thing about me.'

Felt a little stab of pride when Jonny called me his mate. Then I started apologizing again.

'It's all right,' he cried. 'I heard you the first time. 'So why did you close the syndicate?'

'All the fun had just leaked away,' I said. 'And it was bothering everyone too much.'

He nodded. 'Yet that idea was a bit of

gold . . . Still, I'm going to be a bit busier in future. You know that football trial I went to – well I've been called back.'

'Hey, that's excellent. Congratulations.'

'Oh don't start cracking open the champagne yet. Five of us have been called back, but they'll probably only take two. So the tests go on. Still I might just be on my way.'

'I bet your dad's happy.'

'Oh, he can't stop talking about it,' said Jonny. He gave a rather tense smile, then asked, 'Will you do me a small favour?'

'You only have to name it.'

'Ask your sister if she'd like to go to the cinema on Saturday – with me?'

I gaped at him. 'Jonny, I didn't close Chancer because of my sister.'

'I know.'

'So there's absolutely no need to do this.'

'I realize that,' said Jonny. 'I'd just like to . . .'

'But why?'

I don't know, exactly,' he shrugged. 'She's intriguing.'

'No she's not. And I should know, I see her every day.'

'Just ask her, will you?' he said.

'Well I'll try,' I said. 'Only the last couple

of days she's been going around looking like a spat-out Smartie.'

He laughed. 'You make her sound so appealing.' Then he walked away.

So Jonny has actually volunteered to spend a whole evening with my sister. He's clearly gone sensationally mad.

WEDNESDAY MARCH 8TH

9.00 a.m.

NEWSFLASH

I know who the thief is.

Since running the syndicate I've got into this bad habit of arriving at school early. And today I'd just rolled up when I bumped into Lee. He jumped a bit and I sensed he couldn't wait to get away from me, but I just put that down to my magnetic personality – until I reached my locker. It had been broken into again. Only this time nothing had been taken away. Instead, something had been added: an envelope stashed full of money. One hundred and eighty pounds, to be precise.

Remember when I just knew the number of times Twitchy would twitch in a double lesson? Well, in a similar blinding flash I was absolutely certain who'd put that envelope into my locker: Lee.

I chased after him. And I said, 'Thanks very much for returning my money.' I was highly authoritative.

And he immediately burst out. 'I didn't want the money . . . well you can see I haven't touched one penny of it.'

'Yes, I can verify that. So why steal it in the first place?'

'I was just so sick of not winning. Never once did I win so much as an ice cream, let alone any money.' He glared furiously at me as if this was my fault. 'I got so mad that one morning I thought, well no one else will win either. I'm going to sabotage the whole thing. I was inside your locker in seconds by the way. That lock was rubbish.'

'Thanks for the tip,' I replied. 'Do you know, I never once suspected you. You were even the one who suggested everyone be searched. So where did you hide it that day?'

'Down in my shoes. So apologies if the money still whiffs a tiny bit – and for everything else.' He hung his head a bit then. 'I've just been waiting for the right moment to take it back. Been carrying this money around with me all week . . . what are you going to do now?'

'I've got all the cash back,' I said. 'So that's it. Anyway, you weren't yourself. You were in the grip of something bigger . . . gambling fever.'

'Yes, that's exactly what I had,' said Lee. 'An outbreak of gambling fever. I was so desperate to win. It was all I could think about . . . I even had dreams about betting. I didn't win in any of those either.'

'You're over it now though,' I said.

'Definitely,' declared Lee firmly. 'So you won't tell anyone else.'

I shook my head. 'At least you know you've got a bit of a weakness there. So if in later life you find yourself putting loads of bets on horses or dogs or something . . . just stop and remember this conversation.'

'I surely will,' promised Lee. 'Thanks a lot, Harvey . . . be lucky!' Then he stopped. 'I suppose we shouldn't say that to each other any more.'

'I don't see why not,' I replied. 'So, you be lucky too.'

10.45 a.m.
The stolen money has now been returned to all the winners – and I've given George back his 'collection' money too (I hadn't even touched it). People were a bit amazed

about the winnings just popping up in my locker again.

Jonny asked, 'Are you sure you haven't been dipping into your savings?'

'Behave. I haven't got any savings to dip into,' I replied. 'So just enjoy your winnings.'

But Jonny still looked a bit doubtful. Then he asked if I'd put his request to Claudia yet . . .

'I wanted to give you time to reconsider your offer,' I replied. 'I should warn you she's dead miserable at the moment. An evening with her would go very slowly indeed.'

'Just ask her,' said Jonny, 'and do it tonight.'

7.25 p.m.
At seven o'clock the doorbell rang. Dad answered it, then yelled out as if he'd just stabbed his toe. Next he started shouting my name. I sped downstairs, with Claudia right behind me.

'I just found this on the doorstep!' exclaimed Dad. He could have been talking about a stray dog. Instead he was talking about a stray CD player. Mine – which had come home all by itself, apparently.

'I just don't believe it,' I cried.

'And neither do I,' said Dad dryly. Then he gave me this piercing stare. His eyes were like searchlights. 'Can you throw any light on this, Harvey?'

But I was speechless with shock. I really hadn't expected my CD player to turn up like that. It was Claudia who jumped in. 'I think I know what's happened here,' she said. 'The burglar was obviously some young kid who found a house he could break into easily. But ever since he's been full of remorse for his crime. And now he's turned over a new leaf and is returning all his stolen property to their rightful owners.'

I nearly applauded, that was so brilliant. Dad was staring at Claudia now. 'So you think our burglar's trying to make things better?'

'Oh yes,' said Claudia.

'He's obviously quite a thoughtful burglar, deep down,' I piped up.

'Well, let's see if the CD player still works,' said Dad.

And it did. Perfectly.

'He's looked after it so well,' I said.

Then I found a text message from Jonny. It said: *I really couldn't take your CD player and the money. So I'm releasing the CD player back into its natural home. Enjoy!! Jonny.*

7.55 p.m.
Right away I'm going to write down everything Dad's just said, because it's so incredible.

He came into my bedroom and started walking around my returned CD player as if it were a rare archaeological find. He said. 'So tonight we've been visited by a reformed burglar?'

'I really think so,' I said. 'He probably just took my CD player in a moment of madness . . . people can do mad things, can't they?' I went on.

'They certainly can,' said Dad, sitting down on the edge of my bed. 'George wasn't the only one to hide out up a tree. I did exactly the same once.'

'You did?' I gasped, stunned.

Dad seemed to enjoy my amazement. 'I was about your age too. Only in my case it was a tree in our own garden, rather than at school . . . and I stayed up there for a whole morning as well.'

'But why?'

'A very simple reason. I didn't want to go to school.'

My mouth fell open. 'You're joking. You've got to be.'

Dad smiled. 'For a time I was so fed up at school. I seemed to be in trouble all the time . . .'

'Excuse me,' I cried, 'you love school. You're its number one fan.'

'Oh, now I can see what school offers and all the chances I've missed,' said Dad. 'I'm afraid I wasn't always like that.'

'But this is brilliant news,' I continued. 'I thought I was the only idiot in this family. But you're one too. Well, you're not an idiot now, of course. But you were, weren't you?'

'I fear so,' said Dad, bowing his head. 'Now, about this remorseful burglar? You really think he's learned his lesson?'

'Oh, he's seen the error of his ways, without a doubt.'

'And he's not in any trouble at all?'

'Not any more. It's all sorted out. And he's probably reformed for ever.'

Dad got up. 'Well, as I said, I think everyone should be allowed their occasional moment of madness – provided they learn from them. And we both think our burglar has?'

I nodded.

'By the way, Dad, any expenses incurred by the burglary, like the smashed glass in the conservatory, I'd like to pay for.'

'I was hoping you'd volunteer,' he said, then he got up.

I said, 'Some time you'll have to tell me more about your wicked past.'

A little smile formed on his face. 'Some time I just might.'

But I didn't press him any further right then. I think its important to allow parents some privacy.

8.15 p.m.
Claudia was sitting at her desk doing her homework when I tapped very politely on her bedroom door. The flowers had all gone, and there was only one dim light on . . .

'I just wanted to say thanks for your quick thinking earlier.'

She brushed my thanks aside without looking up and returned to her studying.

'And also to tell you that Jonny wondered if you'd like to go to the cinema with him on Saturday.'

She leaped to her feet as if she'd just been scalded. 'What!'

'Jonny just wondered . . .' I repeated, in

a chanting kind of voice, 'if you'd like to go to the . . . ?'

'Be careful,' she cried. 'You're on the thinnest of thin ice now.'

'I know that.'

'You're setting up that syndicate again, aren't you?'

'What are you talking about? This has got nothing to do with that. Honestly. I swear on your life. No – joke. I swear on *my* life. I'm as amazed as you. I told Jonny there was no need to take you out. But for some obscure reason he insisted.'

Claudia's face wobbled with shock. Then she turned away from me. So I said, 'Do you want to have a bit of a think about this? Shall I pop back later?'

'Tell him the answer's no. Definitely no,' she replied in this squeaky voice, and began shaking again.

Although being kind to my sister isn't exactly one of my hobbies, I didn't feel I could leave quite yet.

I said, 'Personally, if I were you, I'd go on Saturday.' I thought she'd tell me to mind my own business. But she didn't. Instead she lifted her head a little as if she wanted to say more.

'I think Jonny really wants to go to the

pictures with you. And he'll pay, so it won't cost you anything. And you do like him . . . and no one can work all the time. Not even you. You're allowed to have some fun bits in life too. I'd even tell Dad and Mum what you're doing on Saturday. They can take it . . .'

I paused. Claudia was watching me intently, her hands gripped tightly together. Suddenly she started walking over to me, after which she did something totally unexpected. She kissed me on the top of my head. Then she whispered, 'Tell Jonny yes.'

I think I might be starting to understand girls.

THURSDAY MARCH 9TH

I delivered Claudia's message to Jonny. He looked so happy when he heard her answer as well.

Mind you, he's the only cheerful ex-Chancer member at the moment. All day they've been complaining venomously about how truly boring school is now, then looking at me in a very accusing way.

Ellen did defend me. I heard her say, 'Stop having a go at Harvey. He worked really hard with Chancer and we all just took him for granted. You can't blame him if he's had enough now.'

Later I thanked her for those kind words and she blushed a little bit.

I said to George, 'I can't help feeling guilty. We had people coming to school hungry for fun. But now it's all over and they haven't got anything to look forward to. No wonder they all look a bit shell-shocked.'

I wished there was something I could do. Yet I really didn't want to bring Chancer back. So what else was there?

FRIDAY MARCH 10TH

1.50 p.m.

Another difficult morning. People aren't moaning so much to me personally. But they still look dead gloomy and fed-up. They've still got the memory of Chancer in their eyes.

And I thought, I've got to do something about this. So at lunchtime George and me decided to try and cheer up our ex-members. We started with Ellen, for no particular reason (and by the way, I don't still fancy her. That's just a silly rumour, which people like me, who are in the public eye, attract).

We said to Ellen, 'We're trying to get this school looking better . . . and you can help.'

'Can I?' she asked. 'How?'

I said, 'Well, we've been observing you – and I have to tell you, you're just not smiling enough. In fact, we were shocked at how little you've been smiling, weren't we, George?'

'Deeply shocked,' he agreed.

'So for the rest of the lunchtime we want you to smile as you walk along. Will you do that for us?'

Ellen stared at us in disbelief. 'You're both mad,' she declared.

'We certainly are, but will you . . . Oh look, George, I think it's started.' We both immediately peered closely at her mouth. 'Yes, a little smile is forming at the corners of her mouth. Now, can you stretch that out a bit more for us, Ellen. Oh, that's just perfect. A smile to be proud of.'

She was actually laughing now.

'Now, will you keep smiling as you walk along?' I asked.

'I might,' she grinned.

Then we rushed up to other glum-looking ex-Chancer members. And soon we were just going up to anyone who looked a bit miserable. By the end of the lunchtime we'd left a trail of grinning – if highly puzzled – people behind us.

I stared after them with a sudden rush of joy. And then I realized something. 'George . . .' I began.

'What?' he demanded.

'I might,' I said slowly, 'have thought of a whole new way to liven up school.'

'That's brilliant news,' said George, in an awed whisper. 'What is it?'

'Now don't rush me, the details are still very hazy. It's just started forming in my head.'

'Yes of course,' said George eagerly. 'Take your time, take as long as you need.'

And even as I write this more ideas are jumping into my head. So I won't even tell you about it yet. But George is coming round to my house tonight for an emergency meeting about this.

8.55 p.m.
I think we've done it. The scheme's still in its very early stages, though.

It's called CLOWNS UNITED (catchy or what) and the idea is to bring FUN into the drabbest day of the week: Monday. (Then, once we've got Monday sorted, we'll move on to Tuesday and so on.)

Every Monday, each member of CLOWNS UNITED has to perform a comedy challenge. The first one is called: MAKE A TEACHER LAUGH. More details to follow.

And what's the prize you ask? Well, listen to this! The prize is like servant-for-a-day only much, much better. We're calling it: Be A V.I.P. FOR A DAY – and this time the winner will have everyone in CLOWNS UNITED waiting on them and getting them out of trouble: Forgotten your P.E. kit? Can't do your homework? Need someone to take the blame for something . . . ? Leave it to CLOWNS UNITED. For one day you rule, but again, more details to follow.

George and me have already texted Chancer members about a special meeting on Monday morning at 8.30 by the school lockers. Chancer members can automatically transfer their membership to CLOWNS UNITED if they wish and everyone's texted back to say they want to do just that. But George and me are having a special planning meeting tomorrow as there's tons more to work out. But I don't care, as I love inventing ways to make school better. In fact, it's just about my favourite hobby now.

And these last few months have been the most exciting of my entire life. It's been great telling you all about it. I'm afraid I've got to close diary down now. But don't dare forget CLOWNS UNITED (copyright © Harvey and George), will you?

Coming to *your* school SOON!!

RESCUING DAD
Pete Johnson

'How do you improve your dad?'

Joe and Claire can see why Mum chucked Dad
out. He looks a mess, he can't cook and he's useless
around the house. Something must be done: they're
the only ones who can help transform him into
'Dad Mark Two'. And when they unveil this new,
improved dad, Mum will be so impressed she'll take
him back on the spot!

But then disaster strikes – Mum starts seeing the
slimy and creepy Roger. And Joe and Claire's plans
take an unexpected turn – with hilarious results.

'Pete Johnson is a wonderful story-teller'
Evening Standard

ISBN 0 440 86457 7

HOW TO TRAIN
YOUR PARENTS
Pete Johnson

They think I'M a big problem.
Wrong. THEY are!

Louis can't handle it any more. His new school is Swotsville and his mum and dad have fallen into some very bad ways. All they seem to care about now is how well he's doing at school (answer: not well) and what after-school clubs he wants to join (answer: none!). They're no longer interested in his jokes (his dream is to be a comedian) and have even nicked the telly out of his bedroom!

What's going on? And can new friend Maddy help? For Maddy tells him her parents used to behave equally badly until she trained them. All parents have to be trained – and she knows a foolproof way . . .

'Peter Johnson has created a boy who makes you laugh out loud' *Sunday Times*

ISBN 0 440 86439 9

TRUST ME,
I'M A TROUBLEMAKER
Pete Johnson

Got called a 'bod' again today. Also a 'stupid creep', a 'suck-up' and 'teacher's pet'.

Archie is twelve but sometimes he acts like he's forty! Maybe it's because he used to live with his gran. Or maybe he's just a natural nerd.

Miranda Jones, class troublemaker, is about to find out. For she's decided that she's going to change Archie – transform him from Total Loser to Troublemaker Extraordinaire.

And Archie wants her help. For surely only troublemaking can scare off Dad's ghastly new girlfriend . . .

'The devastatingly funny Pete Johnson'
Sunday Times

ISBN 0 440 86626 X